A Burnable Town

Philip Davison was born in Dublin in 1957. He has written six previous novels – *The Book-Thief's Heartbeat, Twist and Shout, The Illustrator, The Crooked Man, McKenzie's Friend* and *The Long Suit.* He has also written drama for radio and television. His play, *The Invisible Mending Company*, was performed on the Abbey Theatre's Peacock stage. The television dramatisation of *The Crooked Man*, the first of Philip Davison's Harry Fielding novels, was screened in 2003.

Cavan County Library
Withdrawn Stock

A BURNABLE TOWN

Philip Davison

JONATHAN CAPE
LONDON

CAVAN COUNTY LIBRARY
ACC. No. ...C.l.1.9.6.2.0.9
CLASS No. .... (IR)
INVOICE NO. ...7.0.3.2....
PRICE.... €.13.84

Published by Jonathan Cape 2006

2 4 6 8 10 9 7 5 3 1

Copyright © Philip Davison 2006

Philip Davison has asserted his right under the Copyright, Designs
and Patents Act 1988 to be identified as the author of this work

This book is sold subject to the condition that it shall not,
by way of trade or otherwise, be lent, resold, hired out,
or otherwise circulated without the publisher's prior
consent in any form of binding or cover other than that
in which it is published and without a similar condition
including this condition being imposed on the
subsequent purchaser

First published in Great Britain in 2006 by
Jonathan Cape
Random House, 20 Vauxhall Bridge Road,
London SW1V 2SA

Random House Australia (Pty) Limited
20 Alfred Street, Milsons Point, Sydney,
New South Wales 2061, Australia

Random House New Zealand Limited
18 Poland Road, Glenfield,
Auckland 10, New Zealand

Random House South Africa (Pty) Limited Isle of Houghton,
Corner Boundary Road & Carse O'Gowrie, Houghton, 2198, South Africa

The Random House Group Limited Reg. No. 954009
www.randomhouse.co.uk

A CIP catalogue record for this book
is available from the British Library

ISBN 0-224-0 7117-3

Papers used by Random House are natural,
recyclable products made from wood grown in sustainable forests;
the manufacturing processes conform to the environmental
regulations of the country of origin

Printed and bound in Great Britain by
Mackays of Chatham plc

For Desmond King

In the latter days of the Second World War low-priority urban targets for Allied bombers were designated Burnable Towns.

'Are there any other kind?' I once asked the old man. 'No, son,' he replied.

Part 1

CHAPTER 1

Somewhere somebody drops a pearl into a beaker of vinegar, challenging their companion's eyes as it dissolves, just to make a point. And, just to make sure the point is made, they're going to drink the vinegar.

I know people like that. I've had them look into my eyes. I've learned to break their stare.

Somewhere beyond the realm of thinking this person, this unfinished being, is supremely prepared – but for what? Not for this waiting. This going to ground.

I have also learned that facts do not explain the world, but I will give you the facts relevant to my situation, and I will try to explain.

I was languishing in my room in oppressive heat, not lifting a finger, but my mind was racing. It was going through again and again the same bald facts of my escape so that I might truly have a sense of deliverance. I was still in shock. That made these facts come in a breathless rush.

My fearless apprentice, Johnny Weeks, and I were

hiding out in Spain, after we'd been in a fire fight with a gang of hired assassins in London. We had been given a task as minders. We had our charge in what we were told was one of the firm's safe houses. But our pistols were defective – we'd been duped. The plan was for us, and our charge, to perish in the service of one man's ruthless determination to have his way. The bigger picture, the master plan, was for this man to discredit our controller in chief, Clements, to see him crushed. To take his job. This man was one of the new breed of fanatics in the anti-terrorist fraternity. Their fanaticism, they claimed, exceeded that of the terrorist. Johnny and I were meant to prove fatally inadequate in our serving of an outmoded notion of how Britain might be defended from terrorist attack.

But I found out about the defective guns. Just in time to make it a real fire fight. That is, shots going in both directions.

And, when I went looking for the man responsible for this piece of madness I found him with my ex-wife, Juno. I couldn't do what I wanted to do, which was shoot him. Couldn't do it because she was there. And, because of my hesitation I got a knife in the small of my back. I went to hospital under my own steam. Later, Johnny came to the hospital, gathered me up, and we got out. We went to ground. Two separate bolt-holes in Spanish coastal towns thirty-five miles apart.

Finally, I had to move to keep a rendezvous. I went out into the blazing heat, sat on the appointed bench and tried to suppress what was playing in my head. I was waiting for another of the visits Johnny made to see if I had any news from London. Were we safe? he would want to know. Our mentor gone bad – had he been exposed? Had Clements dealt with our would-be killer, Jack Bradley?

It was just the two of us and Johnny wanted me to think for us both. He hadn't grasped the extent of my trauma. Nor how hard I had to work to function.

Burning on the bench, I watched with peripheral vision a heavy-set man who had sat down adjacent to me in the shade. He wasn't native. He was reshaping his soft white hands in the heat, working each with the other in turn, spreading the flesh, making them larger and thinner in anticipation of catching a cool breeze. I had a strong urge to speak to him. Everything had ground to a halt in my world. I was weary of telling myself how lucky I was to be alive. I had no news from London and I needed to get beyond having to plan a feeble sentence to utter to a stranger.

I should have listened to the voice of the smaller, more sensible self, the one who said there was no such thing as being supremely prepared, and that I ought to know that hot climates didn't suit me for longer than a short week. I had developed a perverse interest in watching the hide of the satchel I had brought tan progressively in the sun.

The fat man on the bench had a megaphone in a well-worn Boots plastic carrier bag. What was he doing with a megaphone? A football match, I thought. But he wore no team colours. There were no big matches to be played in this remote spot. Did he get separated? Was he lost?

Johnny was late. Had he been on time the bench would still be in the shade. I'd broken my pair of sunglasses and was deliberately torturing myself by not replacing them. These were the easy times, my healing mantra would have it. Maybe that's why I felt like weeping.

I couldn't get a clear picture of what was to come. The heat on my face had me thinking I was getting some healing, but my survival kit seemed to comprise one bookie's pencil with which to make more miscalculations. Long odds suddenly seemed attractive.

The fat man turned to me. He had a wide parting in his oiled hair, running up the centre of his head. This is where you cleave this head in half, it said. He had been out in the sun too long and the parting was now a fiery red line. It was like somebody had taken a laser gun to him.

'Terrible, isn't it?' he said in a Scottish accent.

· 'What's that?'

'The heat, man. It's nae joke.'

'Oh, aye.' I pointed to the megaphone in the carrier bag. 'You must be tired dragging that thing around.'

'Oh, aye,' he replied. The retort sounded better coming out of his mouth.

'Football?'

'No.'

'A protest?'

'Nah. I teach kiddies.' He gestured to the broad expanse of sea. 'Swimming. I'm over wi'a group.'

'Oh . . . very good.'

He gave me a hard look. I felt like a fraud.

'It's too hot, but.'

I thought he was speaking in code.

'It is,' I confirmed. Did he want me to suggest we get drunk in a Spanish bar at eleven o'clock in the morning? I would gladly have done so, but I wasn't responding well to the test. I'd made him feel uncomfortable. He rose to his feet.

'Aye, well, nice talking to you,' he said and took his scorched parting and his megaphone out into the sun. He moved slowly. The heat had given him lead feet. The back of his shirt was soaking with sweat. There were beads of sweat on the back of his neck. He wasn't one to mop his brow. He was more resigned to the climate than me.

'Hey,' I shouted after him. 'Is it too early for a heavy beer?'

Evidently it was, because he turned and gave me another hard look before continuing on his way.

The church bell rang. The ringing seemed too light, too feminine for the squat, thick-walled steeple. My old man would have had something to say about that, having been a bell-ringer in his parish church. He would have listened attentively as I did now, but with purpose. With real knowledge.

The ringing ceased. Johnny was an hour late. I tried not to worry. I closed my eyes and walked down the street in south London where I used to live with my wife. She still lives in the house. I could hear my feet tramping the pavement. I could smell the London air. I saw a magpie land on the granite ball that crowned the façade of the terrace. As I approached the door the bird lifted off and with a light push of its claws it made the ball topple. You get that sort of thing happening in a cool temperate climate, I was thinking, what with the explosion of the magpie population and the general dampness. In my daydream I broke my stride and avoided contact with the falling granite ball. I mumbled something about nature not always doing a good job.

Visiting my ex-wife and avoiding falling masonry – these were risks I judged well, I decided. The sun was stewing my brains.

I got up and began to walk. I was suffering from some kind of apnoea, that is to say, there were moments when I involuntarily resisted drawing breath. Most people who are prone to the condition suffer it only in their sleep. I had a daylight waking version. Johnny not showing up was today's trigger. It was something we Fieldings handed down through the generations like old dinner plates. It was our way of offsetting panic. Perhaps in these quiet, desperate days I was also doing it in my sleep.

Don't worry about Johnny, said the small voice. How many times has he been late? Go back to bed. He'll show up and make no apologies. The smaller more sensible self wasn't getting any wiser.

Heavy-footed and light-headed, I advanced on the hot pavement anticipating my own private earth-quake. Soon, I had to pause and take hold of a down-pipe and draw deeply on the broiling, acidic air. That was when I saw Catalina, the caretaker and cleaner in the old apartment block where I was staying. She was striding down the middle of the narrow street that led to our block. She saw me and came over to greet me in her Mexican Spanish. She spoke good English and knew that my Spanish was poor, but she wanted to encourage me.

Catalina had told me my shirts were too big. Twice, we'd gone down to the beach together in the late evening when most people had left and got into the water and played Save Me. I'm not a strong swimmer so, on both occasions, it was me who was saved.

An expression of concern crossed her face. 'Harry,' she said, 'you have too much sun.'

'I know, Catalina.'

'You forgot your hat.'

'I've put it down somewhere.'

Then, to my surprise, she waved her hand once over her head in a dismissive gesture and told me that she never liked that hat, that it didn't suit me, and that I was to buy another in the shop up the street. She would accompany me. We would go there directly.

I accepted her offer and thanked her in Spanish. She was pleased as much with her own effort as she was with my response.

'You were drunk when you left down your hat,' she said.

I denied the charge and even as the words came out of my mouth it occurred to me that her last utterance was an observation, not a question. An observation without reproach.

She took my arm lightly and went with me to the shop. I bought a hat that met with her approval. I didn't much like it myself, but it was two sizes too big and that made it tolerable.

'There,' she said raising a palm and bending her double-jointed fingers in an expressive manner, 'you see, Harry.'

I nodded, but no, I didn't see.

If I drank enough water, steam would come out of the little round metal vents.

She inclined her head. I felt the need to tilt in the opposite direction. It's a piece of geometry that's difficult to get right. She was good at it and could make the moment last while I chose not to recognise her advances.

Get back to the flat. The little voice was louder now. More autocratic. What will Johnny do if he can't find you? He'll do something foolish. The voice was annoying me. It had the burr of God when he's had too much to drink.

The apartment block was up a narrow street with an incline that opened onto a small triangular courtyard, grandly named after a Spanish king. I slowed as I entered the courtyard, looking for Johnny in the shadows. No sign of him. I glanced into the grocer's shop that opened long hours and sold cured meats that were suspect but tasty. Johnny liked that kind of thing. He wasn't in there.

Mrs Espinosa, the woman living on the ground floor, inspected me as I entered the block. She was the closest thing to a concierge our building had, though she denied the role. I knew for a fact that she paid Catalina her retainer, money that came from the building's owner. She regularly complained about my laundry which hung on a little rack fixed to the back balcony. She claimed that it dripped into her son's dinner, which she put out for him on the table in her yard. All right, so there were a few droplets from my laundry, but I had spent some of my idle time watching her bullish son. He was a local government bureaucrat who kept goldfish in a black plastic dustbin in his mother's yard. I think he had a breeding thing going. I'd seen him give this dustbin a good kicking when something wasn't going right for him. He had a role in organising the town festival and had some scheme going here, too. One day I watched him stacking boxes under the stairs in the common area. The following day there was a cheap padlock on the door. I took a peek anyway. It was something to do. What he had in there was a large stash of fireworks.

He was suspicious of me. He liked to translate his mother's complaints into perfect English, even though he knew I could grasp them in Spanish. On the occasions I met him I made a point of greeting him with a big '*Hola*', a smile and a handshake. That really got his goat because, being a local government official, he felt he should respond in kind.

To take my mind off Johnny I thought about boxing Espinosa junior on the nose if I met him on the staircase.

I looked out the small kitchen window at the back. All was quiet. A strong sea breeze the previous night had made the plastic clothes pegs bunch in the middle of the slack line that hung between two Moorish dovecote chimneys. Somebody whistled and I jumped. Nothing came of it. I forced myself to lie down on the bed. Forced some home-spun therapy. I thought of the sheepdog trials on the BBC – the lush green slopes, the cold moist wind, the rain clouds scrolling up from beyond the horizon.

I imagined my old man somewhere behind me saying, without rancour: 'It's nice now, but you just wait.' I had to heed him but I didn't have to reply, because he was dead.

The sun still shone above my father's house in Muswell Hill, and in his television set, which was switched on but played to no one. It didn't matter that he was dead. I was coming to visit; coming to find the safety of his house and his garden. I saw where he'd been digging weeds. The French window was open. He may have been dead but I found him napping on the couch. There was sunlight making its big statement on the living room floor.

I could see through to the kitchen. It was afternoon but the breakfast things were laid out on the table, the cup, the plate and cereal bowl upside down to defeat dust. Many of his cups had handles that had been broken and repaired with a mysterious glue he'd acquired in the dim, distant past.

His hands were clasped over the belt of his thick corduroy trousers which fastened above the stomach. A newspaper was spread across his legs. His sun-tanned face and scrawny brown arms suggested that he was more than content in the shade. The Fielding apnoea exaggerated that contentment. Out in the garden a breeze was lifting the canvas of the deckchair in waves, but he was sleeping the sleep of all aged men. He must have sensed me coming because he opened his eyes as I entered the room, and he was glad to see me. He rose from the couch effortlessly. That was an impressive feat in itself. I should have been suspicious.

'It's the boy,' he said, coming to greet me.

'It's good to see you,' I said.

I should have known I couldn't play the scene through without turning it on its head. He embraced me, and while he did so he asked as he looked over my shoulder expectantly, 'Is Juno with you?'

I didn't dare look. She would probably be there, ready to contribute to the sham. And I knew there was to be no reversal of devaluation between us. I was stuck again, but, the doorbell sounded. The doorbell in my Spanish flat, that is.

I got off the bed slowly because of the wound; quietly, because I wasn't sure it was Johnny.

I picked up the pistol and moved to the door soundlessly. Apnoea has its uses.

CHAPTER 2

When the intercom wasn't working the main door to the apartment block was left unlocked. Visitors came upstairs and knocked on doors. There were no spy holes.

'Yes?'

'Harry, it's Johnny. You should do something about the hall door.'

Now, he wouldn't have added any kind of remark if there was a problem. That is, if there were other unwelcome visitors.

'Johnny . . . you're the apprentice, remember.' I replied. '*I* tell *you* what's what.' Now he knew there was no problem inside the flat, except that he had to face my rage.

I slipped the automatic under the waistband of my trousers. I had bought these baggy trousers for the heat – here was something else I didn't much like. I made a mental note – if Johnny Weeks didn't get us killed, I would either buy a new pair or leave the country for a cool, temperate climate with wet sheep-dogs and green hills.

I opened the door.

There could be no denying Johnny was in his element. It looked as though his face had just been smacked and he felt the better for it.

I manhandled him into the centre of the room.

'Hey,' he said, 'so I'm late.'

'So you're late?' I thumped him hard on the shoulder. It didn't seem to bother him. He was still the better for being smacked about.

'Hey. Any news?'

'Yes. I can see why anybody would want rid of you.'

'Hey, I saved your life.' He was expecting another dig and was ready to roll back on his hips.

'Will you quit that "*Hey*" crap? Will you?'

'I left on time, but –'

'I don't want to know,' I cut in. I looked him up and down to make a point of my disgust, but it didn't register. He was comfortable in his clothes and at ease with the temperature and humidity. He was wearing the snake-skin and canvas shoes he told me a red-haired Majorcan had made for him. He was carrying a large paper envelope with something bulky in it. It was a quality envelope, the sort used by civil servants to send documents from one department to another. He had this under his arm together with a folded *Times* newspaper.

He was in his element, but for all his bravado, he was nervous. He'd developed this chin-stretching habit that I associated with violinists just before they set to playing their instrument. It made me want to break his jaw.

'Are we safe?' he asked.

'I don't know,' I barked. 'So, we take it that we are not. All right?'

'All right.'

On this visit I was going to help him write a letter to his girlfriend. When Johnny wasn't stirring trouble he liked everything to be entirely normal. He had decided that his blandishments were, after all, unclear. He wanted to write his girl, Tina, a letter to ensure clarity where previously there was ambiguity. What could be more temporal than that? I was the one in a permanent state of panic, not Johnny. In truth, I was more likely to put us in jeopardy than my apprentice.

'She isn't even my type,' he had protested, intending to add to the sincerity and credibility of his case.

He'd gone to great lengths to disguise his request for help. He had gone as far as casting me in the role of editor, when, really, he wanted me to write a letter for him to sign. He got it into his head that I had a healthy view on such matters; that I understood his motives better than he did.

'You approach it like a crime,' I had told him, 'that's your problem.'

He was very taken by my observation. It had come as a revelation.

'You do that with all your operations,' I added, and in response he had given an assertive grin. He had offered advice about my situation with my ex-wife and mistakenly read my reserve as an affirmation of his wisdom and understanding.

And now, ironically, since our debacle in London, he was trying to exhibit the particular brand of respect the firm nurtured. If I told him I had observed a man walking on water he would have made no comment but merely asked what stretch of water this was.

'Harry,' he said, breaking into a grin again, 'you got too much sun.' He pointed. 'I bet you look ridiculous in that hat.'

'You think so?'

'Yes, I do.' He plunged his hands into the pockets of his linen jacket and looked about the flat.

'Did you check?' I demanded.

'Yes, I checked.'

'You watched?'

'Yes. I watched.'

Late or not, I needed to be sure he had reconnoitred before entering my building. Any cautionary point had to be hammered home with Apprentice John.

'Hey . . .' he said, growing half an inch.

'Don't "*Hey*" me.'

'I'm looking after us.'

'*You're* looking after us,' I said with a whinny.

'Don't laugh.' There was nothing slack or evasive in his response. He was deadly earnest. That kind of sentiment was touching and just as dangerous as my panicking.

'I could see you didn't want to buy that hat, but you let her bully you, Harry,' he said, just to prove his worth as spy and protector. 'I'm disappointed.'

In my experience smart alecs are destined for untimely decrepitude precisely because of their smartness, but, I predicted, that wouldn't apply to Johnny. He wasn't going to live long.

He was more relaxed now. The power women possessed to make men do things apparently had no effect on the wisdom and understanding a man might bring to a companion's relationship with his girlfriend.

I went to the window, to the outer edge of the curtain, moved it aside sufficiently to allow a clear line of vision down into the triangle. There was a small lizard on my puny balcony. It stood motionless, looking down the drainhole in the corner. Had I spooked it, or was it doing what it normally did? How had it got there?

When lizards closed their eyes the light would go out of the universe. Johnny had read this somewhere and passed the information on to me. Something else he had read about lizards had made a far greater impression on him. This he also passed on as a lesson for us both. He told me that some lizards seized their own tails to prevent themselves from being swallowed whole.

'Nobody followed me,' Johnny said, a little insulted that I saw fit to look.

'We have to be sure,' I mumbled unnecessarily.

The lizard's body didn't move, but one eye swivelled in its socket and fixed on me. I had an urge to whistle for a sheepdog. Fucking dog would have you before you got down that drainhole.

I took in the courtyard again. Nothing exceptional, nothing irregular. There was, of course, the usual dull expectation of the impossible. Around the corner there was a bronze man on a bronze horse. I had been expecting them to make a clumsy entry into the courtyard. Statues make me uneasy. I don't like their smooth, blind eyes. What are they all waiting for?

The shaded side of the statue – I was sure that was

where Apprentice John had lurked before following me into the apartment building.

'I'm hungry,' he said. 'Are you hungry? Let's go out and get something to eat. Something mucky. Something with a bit of heat.'

Johnny was fascinated by dangerous situations and that is a trait not easily abandoned. I should know.

We had met a fortnight previous. He'd travelled the long distance from his hideout to mine and he was hungry then, too. On that occasion we went to a disreputable bar in my not very disreputable town. Local petty criminals, pimps and damaged souls who passed looked in the window as a matter of order to see who of their kind was taking time out. We got drunk on whiskey and Johnny caused a scene with a local man. He didn't like this guy staring and making fun of us with his friends.

I admit I was thinking that there was something not right about the man anyway. He was too tall to be wearing a waistcoat and somehow that made his sniggering at us entirely unacceptable.

The fracas occurred outside the bar, but it was soon stopped by the Spanish cops. Two of them pulled up in their squad car and ordered the local men back into the bar. I had tried to make light of the incident. All smiles and tolerant hand gestures, I took Johnny by the elbow and tried to lead him up the street, but he didn't want to go.

'Do you say something about the law?' one of the cops asked Johnny in a reasonable voice.

A reasonable voice, but I didn't like the angle of his chin.

'Me?' said Johnny, replying in the same considered tone.

'Yes.'

'No.' Johnny shook his head eagerly. I knew there would be more trouble.

'You and your friend need something explained maybe?'

'No,' replied Johnny, 'it's all clear.'

'You look for trouble?'

'Who, us?'

I tried again to get him up the street, but he stood firm.

'Yes,' the cop confirmed. I was taking in his companion, the quiet one. I had him marked as having a short fuse.

'No,' said Johnny.

'Oh,' said the cop, his chin at a higher angle than before and a lot stiffer, 'my mistake. Okay?'

'All clear,' said Johnny.

'Get in the car,' the cop ordered.

'Ah, you don't want us in the car,' I said.

The order was repeated, and there was enough of a difference in tone to compel us to get into the back seat of the squad car. For two men who had gone to ground, it was hardly a good situation.

In the car the cop who hadn't yet spoken clicked his fingers, held out his hand and asked, in Spanish, for identification. I showed him a driver's licence and Johnny gave him a Spanish social welfare card he had arranged for himself.

They took us for a long drive. I kept my mouth shut. Johnny hummed and occasionally mimicked screeching tyres as we drove around a corner. I could tell he was gearing up for a scrap. I sent him a message of restraint with an aggrieved look. He just nodded at the cop I was to tackle if there was a fight. He was happy to go for the meaner of the two. I gave a terse shake of the head to indicate that we were not to engage, but Johnny was blind to this.

The cops said nothing. We didn't know where they were taking us. It wasn't to the station. We were driving out of town, up into the surrounding high ground. It was late afternoon.

About six miles out of town they stopped the car, opened the door and told us to get out. We did as we were told. They took their night sticks out and ordered us to take off our shoes.

It was quite difficult to get them off given that we had both been drinking a lot of whiskey. In any case, we took off our shoes. Johnny insisted on helping me with the laces on mine, help I resisted until I thought we were going to get a belt from one of the night sticks.

The quieter of the two cops barked an order. I didn't understand, but Johnny did.

'Socks. He wants them off, too.'

There was no scrap. Johnny didn't get his chance. The cops picked up our shoes and socks, threw them on the back seat of the squad car and drove away.

The walk back to town in our bare feet was hell. We managed to hitch a lift from an old man driving a vegetable van about a mile and a half from our destination. He saw the pilgrim blisters and cuts on our feet. He was amused. He seemed to know what had happened to us and asked no questions.

We were tired and still drunk. We must have slept half an hour or more, because when I woke we were in the back of the van, parked up a quiet side street. The sliding door had been left open and when I opened my eyes I was confronted with a bank of rotisserie chickens, three-quarters cooked. They were in the window of a neighbourhood restaurant, the smell wafting out from the entrance which was on the sawn-off corner. There was no sign of our good Samaritan. We saw only the stocky, leather-skinned woman with reels of copper hair who was tending the rotisserie. She was staring out the window, but not at us. I got the impression she had already inspected us and lost interest. Her gaze was fixed on two identical marmalade cats with white under-bellies that were sniffing around the drains. There was something more interesting down there than roast chickens.

Where had our good Samaritan gone? Probably to a bar to amuse his cronies at our expense. We deserved as much.

Two weeks later my insteps still pained me from exposure to the sun on that forced march. The blisters had scarcely healed. And now that we were going out again Johnny had the nerve to show concern for my sun-baked head. My pallor, he observed, was like yellow broccoli.

The lizard scampered out of sight. Probably ran up the wall or performed some impossible gliding feat.

I went to the bathroom to splash water on my armpits and face. The water chugged in the tap. I put on a new shirt and an old jacket.

'By the way,' Johnny shouted, 'I got your shoes back.'

He had had the neck to call to the police station and retrieve his snake-skin and canvas shoes, and my pair of worn brogues.

When I came out of the bedroom the shoes were sticking out of the large envelope he had brought. He'd put this on the table together with the two-day old newspaper he was passing on to me.

It was only when I saw him take in the room now with a critical eye that I realised how untidy and cluttered it had become since his last visit. Johnny's scrutiny had me thinking about Catalina. Her care-taking stopped at the door unless you had a separate cleaning agreement with her, and I didn't. I had to admire her because she had made no comment about the state of my rooms; nor had she attempted any spontaneous cleaning.

'Harry,' Johnny said, 'you need to feng shui the shit out of this place.'

I grunted.

'And Harry . . .'

'What?'

'You better wear that hat.'

We left the building separately.

How much trouble were we in? I didn't know, but by any reckoning a knife wound could be taken as a measure of malicious intent. I was lucky to be alive.

Were we still working for MI5? I didn't know the answer to that, in spite of understanding clearly what had happened. Powerful individuals who operate in defence of the realm sometimes need to make a point in order to advance their careers; a few look for blood fulfilment. A display of righteous indignation in the face of a seemingly bloodless patience can have a devastating effect.

It can get you a knife in the gut.

I had become obsessed with Jack Bradley's betrayal of us. And with Juno's affair with him.

It was siesta time. My mouth was dry but I wasn't thinking about a long, cold drink. That would come after something primary, something with a sour edge. I had developed an old man's taste for salt and pickles. A selection of tapas would be a good start, but really, what I wanted was a jar of Branston pickle and a Marmite sandwich.

We met again in a tourist bar run at half speed by a silver-haired man wearing a tight black shirt. Johnny saw me wince when I sat down and that prompted him to break the moratorium on the subject of my wound.

'Are you all right?'

'Yes. I'm all right.' Now, that wasn't entirely true, but we both were amazed at my recovery thus far. The rushed treatment I'd got in England was good, but mine was a life-threatening knife wound. I had since been meticulous in cleaning and dressing it, but I couldn't put my hand inside and mend the damaged tissue.

Catalina had taken me to a spiritual healer in the next town. I was deeply sceptical, but I didn't have to be pitch-forked into the man's open arms.

The windows of his rooms were shut. There was

no air conditioning. The interior was calm, but stuffy, smelling of dead flowers, cinnamon and tobacco. It was sparsely furnished, but lavishly fitted with mighty-patterned carpets, offcuts from an altogether larger, more grand interior.

Catalina watched attentively. Had I asked her to leave me alone with the healer I think she would have ignored me.

I stood in the middle of the room between the two of them, drawing even breaths on the stale air. He barely glanced at my wound. He moved his hands along the contours of whatever force field he saw and he told me I was lucky. I had been born with the *amnios* intact.

Catalina translated the word as 'the Balloon of Mercy'. She mimed as she struggled for the proper medical term in English for the membrane that encloses the foetus in the womb.

I left feeling no better, but, inexplicably, the encounter had stimulated a powerful healing, the forces of which seemed entirely indifferent to my corrosive doubt. Maybe that was why I felt so light-headed here with Johnny now. So stupid. So prosy.

Johnny and I drank two small glasses of chilled red wine each. Drank them in silence. Sitting tight. That was my plan of action. For now, Johnny was sitting tight too, and it was driving him crazy.

I asked about his girl. He was grateful that I broke the silence and started on a broad, philosophical note.

'Fucking is serious,' he said. There was not a trace of crudity in his utterance. Instead, there was a reverential tone to it. He spoke in a way that suggested this was a recent discovery and that it had struck him like a bolt of lightning.

He wanted me to confirm his observation but I was too busy thinking about my own losses to answer immediately.

'It is,' he asserted, unnecessarily.

'It is,' I confirmed. 'It's like music,' I said, trying to be big and generous of spirit; trying to sound like somebody who was quick to delight in others' pleasure. 'Question and answer, Johnny. Question and answer.'

He liked the sound of that.

He turned over a cocktail list and put a cheap biro down on it. Could we rough something out? he asked.

'What you need to say,' I told him without lifting the pen, 'is what you said to me.' I was exaggerating; you might even call it lying, because he hadn't said anything coherent about his relationship with her since we had left London in a hurry.

And so, ignoring the little rats that were running around my boiled brain, I wrote a love letter to my ex-wife and passed it off as the letter Johnny wanted to write to his girl. I was surprised at how appropriate it seemed.

It had his girlfriend's name on it. He could copy it out in his own hand and sign it.

I could feel my skin getting thin. I sewed up the subject. Switched tone. 'So tell me, Johnny,' I said with a cursory nod to his feet, 'was there a large pile of shoes in the police station?'

He told me there was an impressive pile of uncollected shoes on display behind the desk sergeant.

'Can't we make a call to London?' Johnny then asked.

'No. We can't make a call. Not yet.'

I was afraid. That was the truth. Afraid that Clements was no longer in charge, that nobody would credit our account of Bradley's treachery. I had no contingency plan if Jack Bradley answered the phone instead of Clements.

On my way back to the flat I did make a call. I took a chance and rang my ex-wife from a call box. I didn't know what I was going to say. Some vague ex-lover's bleating, I expect, but something that might in the end glean the fate of Bradley. I anticipated a suffocated response. In the event, she did most of the talking. She wanted details of my recovery from the knife wound. The way she put it made her sound like a Casualty Department duty doctor.

She had news for me. It was only when she spoke of this that she was flush with compassion. It had nothing to do with her or Jack. The body of my crooked copper friend, Alfie, had finally been found. His wife Ruth was asking for me.

My ex-wife asked where I was. She knew better, but she asked anyway. Maybe Jack had asked her to do just that if I rang. I put down the handset.

I must have left the hat in the phone booth. I only missed it when I turned into the triangle and the sun, which was setting on the horseman's shoulder up the narrow street, caught me full in the eyes.

CHAPTER 3

Some more facts. I put on the recovered shoes and went for a long walk. Dead men talk, but my friend, Alfie, hadn't said much in a while. I was expecting a great outpouring from him. Some hard intelligence. Some blunt advice about human nature. At the very least to have him berate me for my innocence. My trusting nature. My overdeveloped sense of responsibility.

I couldn't sleep that night. I lay awake in the dark, listening, but nothing came. Early the following morning I traipsed up to the high ground then back down again, chanting Alfie's name out of my ears.

When I finally returned to the flat I was overcome with tiredness. I opened a tin of pears, ate them from the tin with a dessertspoon and drank the lifeless sweet water they came in.

Then, I rang Ruth.

I let out my breath and I shared my grieving for my dead friend with all the rectitude I could muster. It had been a long wait for her to have his death confirmed. She put me to shame with her courageous acceptance of her husband's demise. She told me she

28

was going to sell the house and move in with a friend until she found another place to live. It would be good for both of them, she told me. Her friend needed somebody to share the rent if she was to hold on to her nice flat in Clapham. For Ruth there was a bond from music college days.

Where was I, she wanted to know. When could we meet? I avoided giving a direct answer and she didn't press further. She didn't ask if I would accompany her to identify the body. She didn't ask because Alfie had been too long dead. The identification would have to be done by dental records, or DNA.

'I want to be there with you now, Ruth,' I said, 'but I can't.'

'I understand,' she said. The lightness of her words made me swallow hard.

'I'll be there as soon as I can,' I said. For both of us this vague statement had the brittleness of a blatant lie.

'We'd like that,' she said, meaning herself and Alfie.

When was she going to move? I asked. I couldn't think of anything better to say.

Immediately. Though she had lived in the house without Alfie for a long time, now that she knew he was dead it was impossible to bear the solitude.

In an awkward rush, I told her that she should think about things Alfie might have hidden. He was a horder. He wasn't a man who set up standing orders with the bank. He was fiercely independent, I reminded her. I knew she would recognise this as code for cash, bonds and goods, much of which would not have been come by honestly, or have been declared to Her Majesty's Inspector of Taxes.

'The garden was one of his favourite spots,' I told her. 'Your garden, or the next door neighbour's garden. He wouldn't think twice of hopping over the wall after midnight.' I tried to make a joke of it, but I was serious. 'Alfie was happy to bury just about anything.'

But I was confusing her now with my urgency, and my indiscretion on the telephone. 'I haven't thought about that . . .' she said, and already she was sounding more distant, more heartbroken.

'And remember,' I continued, 'he was a good climber. Look up in the trees. Do all of that after a thorough search of the house. Lift any loose floor-board. Put your hand around the back of the immersion tank.'

Some bright spark might suggest she hire a private detective for a day. 'Don't,' I told her. She wasn't to tell anybody what she was doing. She was to conduct the search herself.

'Oh Harry . . .' she said with a tenderness that gave me goose bumps. That was when I saw I'd virtually finished the bottle I'd been nursing.

Against my better judgement, I decided I would wait no longer for news of deliverance. I was going back to London. My indecision had been swept aside by the need to help Ruth. This private mission of mercy, I decided, would get the smell of cordite out of my nostrils, the smell that had filled the stairwell where Johnny and I confronted the two assassins, the smell that had become the demoralising reek of inaction.

Ruth had been my sometime lover. Had been my Juno substitute. Had knowingly been those things. I owed her.

In truth, being with Ruth was about not being with Juno. Going back to comfort my dead friend's wife was about my failure to deal with Bradley. I would force myself to be daring. I would return at an oblique angle and pick through the wreckage with a renewed clarity. That was my rationale.

I cared deeply about the loss of my friend, Alfie. I could have done with the counsel of a crooked copper. I could have benefited richly from his knowledge of corruption. It was easy to get sentimental. I had to remind myself that he had misjudged at least once and it had cost him his life.

I went to see Johnny. We sat out on the shaded terrace of a restaurant eating sardines and chips – Johnny ate more than his share. He took food off my plate, filled his fork in an aggressive manner. He couldn't conceal his impatience.

'You're going back, aren't you?' he said.

'No,' I lied.

He showed me a photograph of his girlfriend. I had not met her but he'd told me she wore a hearing aid. She was as his scant description had painted her except that she had large ears. It's curious, you don't expect somebody with a hearing aid to have big ears. She was cute, and, judging by the photograph, full of life. The kind who smiles and wriggles and talks a lot in the morning when you're trying to get some sleep.

'That's her,' he said in confidence. 'That's Wing Nut.'

This little shared intimacy was uncharacteristic and touching.

'I'm thinking of going back to London myself, Harry,' he said, and swallowed a large sardine whole.

I wanted him safe. I wanted him to quit the firm and to make a life with Wing Nut. I told him we should both be patient. He sneered. I couldn't fault him for this but I thumped the table with my fist to demand absolute compliance. He liked that.

'All right,' he said, his sneer blasted away by a sudden smile. 'We'll both be patient.' He let his smile shine for the few restaurant customers and staff who had turned to look in response to my banging the table.

Jack Bradley fancied he was part of a new, more ruthless, more effective guard working for the firm, but then so did Johnny. Johnny was going to go after Bradley just as soon as I could bring news of our good standing with the firm. If they had Bradley incarcerated Johnny would pay him a visit. He would find a way in. If Bradley had gone to ground Johnny would hunt him out and kill him. I could live with that, except Johnny would have a lousy plan. He'd be impatient. He wouldn't get close enough. These I counted as facts.

CHAPTER 4

So, back I went. Clear-headed. Surprised by my own boldness. Righteous in the face of caution. I took an indirect route, via Dublin. I crossed by ferry and boarded the night train to London. The smell of public-service disinfectant on the damp air was finally enough to see off the cordite. I looked out into a moonlit landscape. Somewhere on the journey I observed a young man in the section between my carriage and the next. He took an apple from his coat pocket and began to eat it. He was alert for that time of night. Maybe the smell was stronger where he was and that concentrated his mind. He was curious about his fellow passengers. He looked at me twice. He also glanced at my leather satchel, now tanned a strange burned orange colour. His glasses were a tight fit. Maybe he didn't want them sliding on his nose when he looked down, or when he ran, I decided.

He kept eating, scarcely allowing himself time to swallow before the next bite, until there was only the core left. Had somebody seen me disembark? Was he sent to spy on me? If I got up, put the satchel under my arm and walked towards him as if I were drunk would he move away?

We were on old rolling stock. He was able to pull down the window in the door and throw the core out into the wind rush. Then he vanished.

I wasn't afraid. Just a little sleepy. That is not to say I was at ease. I didn't want any apple eaters looking at me.

Sometimes, getting what you want can be unsettling.

I would sleep later in a safe place. Right now, I needed to keep vigilant. I put a little arch in my back. Where were all those apple trees that were supposed to grow in the hedgerows from the cores people threw out of car and train windows?

There was no answer. Instead, I experienced an acidic tingling around the damaged tissue of my wound. Was this the undoing of good work, I wondered, or simply a cold climate asserting itself?

No answer to that, either.

I thought about the little bump on my ex-wife's nose. I often think about that. When we were still together I had broken her nose in my sleep. In my unconscious state I had brought my fist down on it. I can't remember what kind of monster had caught up with me.

Juno was very forgiving.

My practice of summoning this memory has a purpose. Regret usually brings a measure of calm.

In spite of my best efforts on this occasion, I fell asleep.

For a short time.

I dreamt I was hanging out of my Balloon of

Mercy, which was airborne and had expanded to the dimensions of a hot-air balloon. I was making an emergency landing. Drifting ever more rapidly across suburban gardens, getting smacked in the face by the outer extremities of wet branches with razor-sharp leaves. It was a struggle to keep my feet raised sufficiently to avoid collision with a succession of walls and fences.

The wind rush burned my ears. My arms ached. My grip on the neck of the slimy membrane weakened with each minute adjustment in altitude, but I was determined to keep my mouth shut and my eyes open.

As I approached the long grass of my father's overgrown garden I swung my legs up to avoid catching on the neighbour's clothes line. The effort required was enough to send me soaring. I began to lose grip. My wound opened and the tripes gave out. The spirit medicine of Catalina's healer friend drained into the ether.

Then, there was a squeal of brakes and my lolling head fell firmly back onto the headrest of my railway seat. The platform slowed outside the window. The few figures who were in the station at that early hour gathered speed until they were behaving normally and, reassuringly, showed no interest in my arrival.

I opened my hands and spread my fingers along my thighs. Cramp gave way to pins and needles. I had arrived safely in London. However, I got out onto the platform and even before I reached the concourse I could see station security was intense. Armed police were moving slowly and attentively, or were standing to. I glanced at a newspaper headline:

LONDON SEARCH FOR BOMBER.

For a moment, I thought about the firm, about service rosters and the smell that comes from the backs of computers that are never turned off. I wanted to be part of the hunt, but I had to remind myself I wasn't on any service roster; that I was imagining the hot computer smell because I had never been let near any of the firm's computers. For now, I would have to content myself with being the good and alert citizen.

And that I didn't like.

I chose a small three-star hotel. I got a room on the third floor overlooking a private square and slept most of that first day with the window open, letting in the sheet-anchor sound of traffic on the cold air.

I woke late in the evening with a shiver. The arm I had over the cover was a slab of meat; the other was numbed from being too long crooked in one position under my head. I took the cold arm inside to warm it up before getting to my feet and going to the window.

London. And all that it could bring.

It had been raining. A smell of wet tarmac drifted up from the street. There was a line of mature beech trees spreading over the park railings, over the pavement and the parking spaces. There were life-sized, solid wooden owls hung from wires high in the branches to keep the pigeons away. The parked cars below were free of pigeon shit.

The owls swung gently in the breeze. Their small pointed ears and hunched shoulders were nicely rigid when they rotated a few degrees in either direction, depending on the wind.

The owl directly across the street seemed to be an exception. It scarcely moved. It just stared at me. I could have been so easily irked by these lumps of wood, but I didn't let them bother me. I could have closed the curtains on them, but instead, I picked them out, greeting each in turn like the objects in my Spanish flat. I bid the one directly across the street to watch over me.

I hooted under my breath.

Then I lay in the bath listening to a Radio 4 play about an English couple breaking up on a visit to Bombay. I listened until the water got cold. Then I went out for a walk.

The walk was more involved than I had planned. Nothing like revisiting old transgressions to get your bearings. And so it was that I found myself in the small hours standing in Alfie and Ruth's back garden. I could see that the house was empty – she'd already moved out.

I stood there taking in the logic of Alfie's garden. The cold wind filled my ears and nostrils. It lifted the hairs on the back of my hands. There was a stand of Dutch elms by the rear boundary fence through which I could see patches of blue night sky. Alfie had told me a long time back that these were diseased trees, they were being eaten away from the inside, but he hadn't the heart to cut them down. Ruth didn't know about the tree disease and he had never told her. I stared up at the clefts in the silhouetted branches of these trees that had outlived my friend. Nice fellow, Alfie, they seemed to say, but you wouldn't want to meet him.

I studied the black soil of the flower beds. I looked over the walls at the neighbours' gardens on either side.

Alfie, where should a friend dig?

The last time I stood self-consciously outside a window in the dark I was doing a favour for a neighbour; I was looking to scare off the shadowy figure she'd seen lurking outside her bedroom. I never did tell her that I was the interloper. I was too embarrassed; too interested in her to admit to my sneaky side, the extent of which never ceases to surprise me.

Dig there, Alfie said, breaking his long silence.

'There,' I whispered, confirming the spot. 'And what about over here?' I asked, turning to my left some sixty degrees and fixing on a spot beside the oil tank for the central heating. That's where I'd bury goods, I thought. No tree roots or awkward bushes, but a nice tangle of creeper that could be easily dressed back in place. In by the wall. Covered from the immediate neighbour's view by the tank.

Alfie wouldn't say.

There were possibilities over the wall, too.

What should I look for, Alfie?

No answer. Answering would make me an accessory.

★　　★　　★

38

There was an envelope on the pillow of my bed in the hotel when I returned. Putting it on the pillow rather than sliding it under the door was a way of letting me know that I was fully in the light, and, incidentally, that a comprehensive search of the room had been conducted.

So. They knew I was back in London. It had taken them less time than I anticipated, and I had assumed they would be on to me quickly.

I inspected the letter closely without touching it. Then, I lay down beside it and stared up at the ceiling. Had Apprentice John inadvertently betrayed us? Or was it my own clumsiness?

That didn't matter now. Contact. That's what I wanted, wasn't it? I couldn't bear being defunct any longer.

Eventually, I opened the envelope. It was from Clements. I could hear him speaking the words as I read them. Inscrutable as ever, I could see him wanting to rub his belly while he listened to the sound of his own voice:

Harry,

Welcome home. You'll want to catch up, no doubt. Be assured I am appraised of the facts. You have shown great character. You have performed a small miracle and I'll not forget that. I want you to know that you and Johnny are in the good books. I have work for you.

He gave me a number to ring and signed off as 'C'.

Clements believed in small miracles. The suicide

who changes his mind on the way down survives to pick himself up and limp to the hospital.

The sounds and smells of a new day told me this was the time in any day when suicides who had changed their minds *after* impact nonetheless managed resurrection. That's what I was thinking as I got up from the bed and went to the window to look at my wooden owl.

I didn't bother to check if I was being watched. I thought I might find my owl blinking furiously to alert me to an intruder, but it was just staring at me.

I could have rung Johnny in Spain to tell him that Clements, personally, had absolved and blessed us. But I didn't. Instead, I hooted softly into the palm of my hand.

CHAPTER 5

I was ravenous. The realisation was quite sudden.

In the steak house I caught a man sitting across the way watching me. I was wolfing my food, as if I hadn't eaten in a week. I wanted to weep. I didn't know why. I kept on eating. Eating at the same pace, but now it was choking me.

It was good to be back in London, but I was scared. I needed to sit here for a time with what was left of my steak and chips and stay still and not get sick.

I rang Ruth's mobile phone number early the following morning.

'Ruth?'

'Oh Harry . . .'

'I'm back in London.'

'I'll be seeing him this morning.' She meant seeing the box.

'I'll come with you.'

'Please come with me,' she said, as though she hadn't heard me.'

'I will.'

'I've to see him at eleven o'clock.'

'We'll be there on time. Don't worry.'

Her friend in Clapham had taken the day off work to accompany her to the hospital chapel. I told Ruth that it would be better if it was just the two of us. I was being selfish. I didn't know how much time I could get with Ruth on her own. Perhaps very little, but enough to stand over our illicit affair. To carry through on it.

'You will come, Harry?' she asked, still not convinced of my reliability.

'I will.'

'He'll be glad.'

'I know.'

I took down the address in Clapham and made an arrangement with her. My head was thumping. I drank a lot of water and had a slow, close shave before going out onto the street.

Well, Alfie.

Well, Harry.

We will have to count this as a good day, all things considered.

We will.

Are you moving in on my wife, old pal?

Alfie, how could you say that? I just didn't believe he could see into the past; that he could read my private desires without my revealing them to him.

Go right ahead. I'd like that if she would. Would she like that, Harry? You can tell me. Whisper it in my ear when she's bawling over my carcass. Bury me in the garden. No marker needed.

I asked if he had any intelligence on my true standing with the firm.

There was no reply. I left the channel open.

I had to be quite forceful with Ruth's friend, who was determined to be supportive. It wasn't an identification, though Ruth persisted in calling it one. Alfie's body had been formally identified through DNA. His police colleagues had seen to that. Too much time had passed to allow for a visual identification by next of kin. He'd been moved from the hospital morgue to the chapel and Ruth was going to accompany him on his journey to the funeral home. She wanted to do that. She had spent enough time without him.

'Ruth,' I reminded her as gently as I could after I had dissuaded the friend, 'you don't have to identify Alfie. That's been done.'

'I have to go there at eleven o'clock,' she repeated.

'Yes. But not to make an identification.'

'But, I'm his wife. I can do it. I can look at him.'

I couldn't bring myself to contradict her. She was breaking my heart. 'Of course you can. We could do it together.'

She was reassured by that.

CHAPTER 6

So, back I was. With a job offer from the controller-in-chief of the firm. I counted myself as one of Clements's small miracles. For now, there was no further talk of Johnny. That suited me. I wanted him out – for his own sake.

I got a message to him. An instruction coupled with a little lie – *Stay put. Nothing yet clear.* It wouldn't be clear for a long time, and then I would tell him he'd been made redundant.

The search for the suitcase bomb brought good weather out of season. It made the sun shine and birds sing. It fostered a cold simple wonder about human nature, clocks and timers. The power of an unexploded bomb got policemen out of bed early and made them more vigilant. It made SAS men play more with their children. It made model citizens of terrorists.

There was no bigger job than this for the firm. The first morning I went in, the pile was buzzing with the hunt for the bomber, but as usual, everybody seemed to know precisely what they were doing, their skill and powers of concentration rendered heroic by an indifferent cosmos.

No specific task was given to Harry. I was made to feel out of the loop. I was to demonstrate heroic humility in my new post of Personal Assistant to Mr Clements.

There was no such post.

Yes, but this was MI5.

What was Harry doing? I was getting cosy with my boss. He was getting me settled in. And what had happened to Jack Bradley? Clements wouldn't say and I wasn't to enquire further.

You didn't want to call Clements by his Christian name. It would sound too much like pleading. Unless invited, of course, and if invited you would be suspicious.

Son of an evangelical minister, was my thought. See the light, son, and the young Clements saw the light but vowed never to speak of it. Probably didn't do spectacularly well at public school and protected himself by being aloof.

Clements didn't like rudeness of any kind. Coughing and facial tics he took to be rudeness, but no amount of crude talk, twitching or spluttering would deflect his wet, archangel's glare.

His mouth was narrow and deep cut, done with a carpenter's chisel. It was a suitably sculpted aperture with perfect joinery for the rich, crafted voice it let out. He had been working on that voice for years. Laughter was a rare thing with him so far as I knew, but when he let that out it sounded as if it was prerecorded and belonged to somebody else.

The mouth was the mouth of an actor, but the eyes were the eyes of a master spy.

Clements was getting grumpy in his old age, and that probably came from a desire to get things right. He had acquired a new mode of under-emphasis with his rich voice. It was a filed-down bark which he used for pointing out important business. He used this now to good effect talking about putting things right for me.

Soap in three languages.

'Harry . . .'

'Yes, Mr Clements?'

'You can call me Anthony when we are not in company.'

Fuck.

'Yes. Thank you, Anthony,' I said, careful not to flinch or clear my throat. I'd be reverting to 'Mr Clements' as soon as possible.

'Good . . .'

He was going to get me the best medical treatment available. A consultant. A panel of consultants, if necessary. No expense spared. Nothing was too good for Harry Fielding. Soap in three languages in my hotel bathroom.

What I got was another standard medical examination from the same spook doctor.

A dirty bomb might at any minute explode in the centre of our great city but I stood resolutely in the same empty waiting room, with its oval-backed rosewood chairs, one at each of the two tall windows. There was the smell of stale cigar smoke. The ticking clock on the mantelpiece seemed to be operating at three-quarters speed.

'Mr Fielding?' the voice said from behind me.

'Yes.' I turned sharply. I hadn't heard him crossing the floor beyond the door. I felt I had already failed some test. I hated this carry-on but in truth I was desperate to belong to the firm. To do Clements's bidding; to reward his faith in me and to be manipulated for the greater good. I wanted to be part of Clements's regime in spite of the Jack Bradleys of this world. If that meant letting this doctor poke my balls and such, so be it.

'This way, please,' the doctor said. It didn't bother him that he had kept me waiting.

I knew where his surgery was, so I marched on. 'Here we are again, Doctor Robert,' I said, 'wasting more of your valuable time.'

He ignored my comment. He was behaving as though it were my first appointment with him. I was going to quote a few lines from the Beatles song, 'Doctor Robert', as I had done last time, just to get him to acknowledge that this was a repeat visit, but he stepped in front of me and made a point of leading the way. 'I've been told you have a knife wound that is now healed,' he said over his shoulder.

'Yes,' I replied. I wanted to tell him we were all about to be blown to bits, but I just knew he wouldn't take any notice.

'This way,' he repeated. He led me to a room adjoining his surgery where there was an ancient X-ray cabinet. I took off my jacket and shirt and stood in as ordered. He stood well back when he triggered the machine from a button box at the end of a long cable.

'You can put your shirt on again,' he said when he'd finished. 'No need to button it.'

He asked no questions about the stabbing.

'This way,' he said again, and led me through a connecting door to his surgery. I assumed I wouldn't hear anything about the X-ray results either, unless there were complications.

'Please,' he said, pointing to the chair in front of his desk, 'sit down there.'

'Thank you.'

'You've filled out the questionnaire?' he asked, easing himself into his own chair.

'Well, you already have that, so I didn't.'

'You didn't fill out the questionnaire,' he said, somewhat indignant.

'You already have it in the files,' I insisted.

He pulled out a drawer, snatched a form from a pile and put it down in front of me. 'Fill out the questionnaire, Mr Fielding, please.'

So, I filled out the questionnaire. Again. Then I went upstairs to piss in a plastic cup. I imagined Doctor Robert downstairs at his desk, scratching a note with his leaky fountain pen on the margin of this new questionnaire – *Thinks he's worth saving* – though I had given him no such intelligence.

When I came back he conducted an instant test on the contents of the cup which, I think, was just for show. He declared himself satisfied with the result. He took my blood pressure, listened to my chest and my back with his stethoscope, examined my ears, and tested my colour vision with cards. He checked my limbs for track marks. He used his

48

rubber hammer on my joints. Then he told me to undo my trousers.

'Do you think they'll pay for a better class of suit?' I asked. 'I'm being promoted.'

'A new suit boosts one's confidence,' he said dryly.

He announced in a perfunctory manner that he was now going to examine my testicles. He mumbled 'Sorry'. I reminded myself I was being born again to the firm.

'Not much more wear and tear since I saw you last,' I said.

He paid no heed.

'Right,' he said, 'you can get up and stand over there.' He pointed to a specific spot and went to wash his hands.

He had positioned me there for the eye-test. He had his back to me at the handbasin. Last time I'd done this I took a few neat steps closer to the chart to read the smaller lines, just to smooth the way. When I turned I had found him watching me in the mirror above the sink. There had been nothing dis-approving in his expression. Another box had been favourably ticked, I was sure.

This time, I didn't take a few steps forwards because I had already taken a quick glance at the smaller lines on the card on the way in and had been caught again. Was he going to ignore that as well? He was looking at me in his mirror with renewed interest.

He came away from the sink. 'Right,' he said. 'From the top.' I was expecting him to turn over the card, as he had done before. But he didn't. 'From the top, please, Mr Fielding.'

I did as I was told. I read aloud down through the letters.

I thought that was the end of it. That was how it had finished before, but after the basic eye-test he remained staring at me intently for a moment, as though he had read something in the pallor of my skin, or in the movement of my eyes. I think he just wanted to conclude his amnesic game with a flourish.

'Your adrenalin level is too high,' he said.

'Really?' I replied. 'And what does that mean?'

'You're in a constant state of readiness – fight or flight.'

He was deliberately letting the knicker elastic of his special brief show.

'I've had a spot of trouble since I saw you last,' I said, pointing to the obvious with my thumb. 'A constant state of readiness,' I said, 'is no bad thing, right?'

He just looked at me.

'And, by the way,' I added resentfully, 'it still gives a lot of pain.' That wasn't true. Not since I'd gone to the healer, but I wasn't going to tell him that. Volunteering such information to a spook quack might break the spell and bring back the pain with a vengeance.

He kept staring at me. He ignored my protest about his apparent lack of attention to my stab wound. He knew I was lying.

'You're relying too much on sugar,' he said. He recommended regular baths, a quick sprint or session with a punchbag once a day. I told him I kept very mixed company and could start a fight on the way home most nights, if needed.

I asked Doctor Robert if he had heard about the

Norwegian key nap. I had just read about it standing at the magazine rack in a newsagent's.

No. He hadn't.

So, I explained. The stressed person finds a quiet office with a chair, sits back and shuts his eyes, but holds his keys out in one hand. He naps until the keys drop from his hand and wake him. Even this short time out is of benefit, the article reported.

Doctor Robert's stare modified just enough to allow for some mock pity. 'You'll have to do better than that,' he told me.

He led me downstairs to the hall. When he'd closed the front door behind me I stood for a moment under a lamp, the globe of which was one-third filled with rain water. The last time I was here it had been one-quarter full. The water was catching the sunlight now. I had an urge to find a stone to throw at it. Must have been the adrenalin.

CHAPTER 7

I was rooting for the key to the office I'd been allocated when I saw Clements being stopped in the corridor by a man in a short-sleeved shirt. It was another of the short-exchange power plays you could see in the pile on any given day. I'm with you, they say, not in so many words. You can count on me. I'll watch your back. Then, they hurry away as if to avoid the embarrassing incident that is sure to occur were they to stay a moment longer.

This one hurried in my direction. I turned the key in the door, entered my office and suddenly he was in behind me, like a prowling cat silently stepping through railings. He had hairy arms and wore a diver's watch. He was wearing glasses with heavy black frames. His eyelashes scraped the inside of the lenses. His ears must have been too far back on his head.

And who are you? is almost always a good question if you don't like the look of an intrusive or quizzical stranger. Beginning with 'And' is important. It shows a healthy disdain.

'And who are you?' I asked.

'I'm the man from downstairs,' he replied, his voice as dry as a cuckoo call. He used the long vowels of received pronunciation. 'You wanted this,' he said, producing a document from a sheaf of papers. 'Sorry, you should have got it sooner. Pensions are up a bit of a heap, too.'

I took the document. There it was. From HM's printing works. The Official Secrets Act.

I wanted this, he had said. Did I? I'd forgotten about the formal business of signing up. About being official. Obviously, everybody in the firm was subjected to the same purifying vapour. Everybody signed up. We were all required to positively welcome the initial infusion of state-induced panic – that was healthy. Received wisdom had it that the panic was always followed by a brief, soothing period of settling and feeling foolish for having given it any thought. I had an incongruous memory-flash of the mouse I found in my trousers on the floor in Spain. Had I not disturbed it in time it might have chewed its way through my fold of bank notes.

'I'll drop by later,' said the hairy-armed man. I didn't actually see him go. He seemed to just disappear.

I got a bad taste in my mouth as I dutifully began to read. Now why was I blocking any rational debate on the matter? It wouldn't be right if I didn't feel uncomfortable signing. I stopped reading. What on earth was I reading for?

Suddenly, I was acutely aware of my own discomfort. My fingers didn't extend far enough beyond the cuffs of my coat. I could feel myself trying to stretch my arms before I reached to an inside pocket for my pen.

I signed it standing up. I gave out with a twisted guffaw thinking of all that I had seen and done unofficially in the name of the firm. Give me a form to fill out or a document to sign and I automatically take on a false persona. These people must know that about me, I assumed, so with the firm's personnel department I only lie a little. More or less at random.

For instance, this was just an approximation of my signature. That is to say, I didn't quite get it right on the first attempt. What was I to do? Sign again underneath?

Everything is a secret to a mouse, remember that, Harry, I might have muttered into one of my overlong coat sleeves. I really can't recall. Nor do I remember the actual scrawling on the paper on the line provided. I just remember watching the ink take a long time to dry.

When the hairy-armed man from downstairs returned some time later to collect the signed document, he behaved altogether like a different person now that I was in his club. He dropped the formal reserve and was full of easy smiles. I soon came to recognise his annoying tactic of pretending to be surprised by the normal and intrigued by all that was mundane. It made him stand out among colleagues who, under constant pressure, led their lives in the immediate future. This special kind of patience suggested that his mind was always clear and he could be relied upon to be a font of common sense and good judgement, which, after all, was a useful trait for a man from Personnel. Furthermore, he wanted you to know that he enjoyed playing up his role. It would be just one of many effective variations on the smoke screen to which I would be introduced in my new post.

'Very good,' he said, making a point of studying my signature appreciatively. 'You have my extension number?' he asked.

'It'll be in the internal directory, won't it?'

'Of course it will.'

I had a mind to ring him and ask for a bed that folded into the wall.

'Now look, Harry,' he said, 'any wasps in your jam, you tell me.'

I couldn't believe he said that. Was he mocking me? 'Right. I'll do that.'

His demeanour seemed to suggest that in the end social cohesion might save us all.

My cynicism didn't penetrate. He gave me a Scout master's handshake before leaving the room.

There was a lot of handshaking that went with this new job, and no two were the same.

So, I had what I wanted. I was safe. I was in from the cold. I was working for a man I respected. I could get back the confidence that had deserted me since the killing of the assassins and my stabbing. The confidence Clements seemed to think was still there. I would break for ever with Juno and hereafter be a model spook privy to the whole truth, known only to the inner circle. I would be permanently elevated above the fog.

I was safe, wasn't I?

CHAPTER 8

That same night the weather turned cold and London got a break. A copper on the beat grew suspicious of a nervous man with a car that wouldn't start. What was I doing while the bomber was being taken into custody?

I was lying wide awake in my hotel bedroom.

Sleeping was getting to be like waking time. The converse was more disturbing. I needed to camp in objective dark, to soothe my own breast, to quell my shot nerves. I needed to separate sleeping from the waking state with a period of rest. I needed to rest as wild animals rest. That was what I was thinking when the call came from Clements.

I ran all the way.

In the firm's underground garage Clements introduced me to a tall man who stood disturbingly close in an attempt, it seemed, to counter an urge to capsize and cause damage.

Richard Baldwin. He and Clements had been talking behind others' backs. I could tell. Gossip.

Secrets of the inner sanctum. Clements had got the better of him, I speculated. That was the protocol.

'Hello, Mr Baldwin.'

'Good morning, Harry.'

Now why was I thinking he had already got the better of me? Christ. It was me they had been talking about, was it?

'Deputy in charge of Internal Security,' Clements announced with a hint of mockery.

'Ah,' I managed.

'Deputy Plod,' Baldwin said helpfully. He also managed to convey with his tone and posture that he had observed the unlucky tread of a stab victim in the corridor and that it had been duly noted.

'I've looked at the file he keeps on you, of course,' Clements said after he and I had moved on. 'It goes back quite some time.' He sounded surprised. 'He has you down as a solitary forager and black-out drunk.' He didn't sound surprised.

'Does he?' I tried to be professional, that is to say, I tried not to take offence. Clements had one mouse-hair eyebrow mischievously raised to encourage my professionalism. 'Well, then, there's a chance they might leave me alone.'

The eyebrow came down a notch. Surely I wasn't about to make so obvious a miscalculation. He shook his head. 'The best we can hope for is that you'll be labelled untrustworthy.'

'The best?'

'That just leaves me to trust you, doesn't it?'

'Yes. Yes, it does.'

'Good. I'm glad we've got that straight.'

In this alabaster palace there was always a use for men and women with their sides kicked in. I knew that.

Clements was deeply introspective on route to Paddington Green. Discontented in a philosophical way. I wound down my window a little. Winding down the window seemed to be a terribly destructive act, but there was a sweet putty smell coming from Malcolm that was annoying me. Malcolm was one of the firm's more eager chaps.

Nothing was said for some time. I listened to the sounds of London and wondered about nothing in particular. These were familiar sounds, clearing a channel for something unfamiliar – namely the voice of a man telling his interrogators why it was that he would want to plant a bomb. That is, if he would utter any sound at all.

Clements was gazing up at the overcast sky, measuring it, it seemed, for some grand plan. Dividing it into manageable blocks or a working grid, inviting any giddy opportunist who might be watching to say that he could do with a piece himself if there was any to be had.

'Mr Clements,' I said, 'is that window too cold for you?'

'No. Thank you, Harry.'

I took it as confirmation that my boss was up with his measuring tape in the clouds. 'Because, if it is, I can close it straight away. I don't mind.'

I caught Malcolm's hooded glance in the rearview

mirror. He applied more thumb pressure to the steering wheel. He thought I was being facetious. Hey, Malcolm, I'm deadly serious, I wanted to say. I wound down the window because of your exotic aftershave. You can fuck right off looking at me like that.

'We'll go round the back, sir,' Malcolm said, though we were still some distance from the station. It was an unnecessary statement. Of course we were going in by the back. Clements barely acknowledged with a nod. Now, Malcolm was annoyed with himself too. Clements's silence had made us both uncomfortable.

We entered the police station where we were met by two senior detectives. Clements didn't pay them much attention, nor did he look around him. Instead he sniffed the air. 'Smells of the lion house,' he commented to me in a loud theatrical aside and moved on. He seemed to know where he was going.

'Excuse me, sir,' said the most junior of the detectives to Clements, 'I think I should warn you. There's a bit of a whiff in there.'

'I did rather notice,' said Clements.

'No, sir. In there. In the interrogation room.'

'Really?' said Clements. 'Worse than out here?'

'It's him, sir. The suspect. Not much we can do about it.'

'Right. Well, thank you for the warning, Detective.'

'Very good, sir. Would you like to see him first, before you go in?'

'Yes. I would.'

Clements stood for a long time staring at the man through the two-way mirror. The same brooding silence he had fallen into in the car was manifest here, on both sides of the glass. The man was sitting on a chair, being watched by two senior Special Branch detectives and the court-appointed solicitor.

I didn't want to sit, so I stood around, feeling the strain at my knees and in the small of my back. I was getting an unpleasant tingling around the damaged tissue of my wound which I tried to ignore.

Clements's patience was absolute. He was like an old tree that would gradually lift a slab of pavement, or break apart a tree house with its growing. To hell with that, I was thinking. Then he spoke from his deep, dark cavern. Such was these people's ambition, he said, that they would claim to have delivered a bomb that had moral purpose; the attack brokered as a deadly and violent ritual, a way of stimulating, but also managing, change.

It was this notion of managing change, he told us, that we must target. Disrupt this notion and the cloak of invisibility falls away. The terrorist is exposed by his immoral actions. He would be encouraged to fight his cause through politics and trade. He might even be won over by the idea of small acts of humanity punctuating the usual dirty business of collective human endeavour. Swapping hatred for dislike was always a step in the right direction. Mistrust was better than no trust at all. Let the children grow up around a table. Give them food, prosperity and culture. Above all – eloquentia. Give them language.

Malcolm and I both nodded, knowing that no amount of nodding would be enough.

'You want me to sweat the bastard, Mr Clements?' Malcolm asked. It was meant as a joke, but really he fancied he would be as effective as any of the firm's inquisitors, who, incidentally, would soon have their chance now that the police had done the ground-work. As in the car, Malcolm felt he had to say some-thing. And, it must be acknowledged, Malcolm could indeed have sweated the suspect. It was said in jest, but not taken as such because, evidently, Malcolm hadn't really been listening.

Clements broke his stare for the first time to look at my rash colleague. 'No. Thank you, Malcolm.' The measure of intolerance in his tone, and its sudden-ness, surprised me.

Special Branch detectives had already put the direct questions to the suspect many times – Where was it to be planted? Was there more than one suitcase or parcel? Who were his support team? His contacts? The time and exact place of detonation? When was he to set the timer? We were all assuming he didn't know that the instant the timer switch was engaged was the moment of detonation. The donkey would be blown to bits along with everything else in range.

The suspect had offered no meaningful response. I assumed Clements himself wanted to use some sensitive information the firm had to loosen his lips. We had something, I knew. Sketchy details of this man's youth. Names of early associates. But nothing of consequence so far as the firm's analysts could tell.

We got the smell the moment we entered the room.

It was not overbearing, but there was no escaping it. Sour, fusty and dispersed so as to be rubbing against all four walls evenly. I assumed we weren't supposed to react. Certainly Clements ignored it.

His interrogation technique was legendary in the service, but legends weren't to be taken at face value, particularly in MI5. I was glad to get the chance to observe first hand. From the outset, he was conspicuously patient, polite, preferring to be in another more interesting place, but dutifully engaged in the sacred, if joyless, job of detection.

It became clear to me that Clements had no interest in the sensibilities of the guilty or the innocent, and this was a revelation. A real lesson. A man might be wearing a pin-striped suit and bowler hat, or a rag on his head and Kevlar body armour, and it would appear to offer him no clue. He would comment on the tectonic fault lines in the human soul before he asked for the name of a man's tailor or how it was the subject came to be wearing body armour. Equally, there would be no ambiguity about his objective, his uniformity of purpose. He seemed to promise that with his brand of ethical socialism the public realm would never be shut out. No ultimatums would be issued. Rather, they would be understood. He let it be known that he refused to believe that any man he interrogated was lacking in cognisance or mental ability.

Which made this encounter interesting, because this one was clever at playing thick. He was well dressed, in spite of the smell. In fact, he was dressed better than me. I made a mental note to take up Clements's offer of the firm paying for a good suit.

He sat rigidly, with his arms folded and legs crossed. I was glad to see his suit was a little short on the sleeves. I could see two faint lines where the legs had been let down. He had a white handkerchief folded in the breast pocket, which struck me as curiously old-fashioned for a man with a suitcase bomb. The top button of his shirt was closed. The coppers had his tie and laces. His shoes were polished but worn down from a lot of walking. He was wearing a pair of those expensive see-through socks. He wouldn't have looked out of place among a clutch of bachelor civil servants in the Ministry of Education canteen.

Being as well dressed as him wouldn't suffice, I decided. I'd have to get something better.

The jowly solicitor just stood in the corner holding one hand with the other and watched with large, wet, pearly eyes.

It was some time before Clements spoke. He stood to one side of the cheap office desk and rummaged in his pockets distractedly. The subject made no bones about staring. To my surprise, Clements produced a packet of cigarettes. He took one out and brought it up to light, stopping short of his jaw. His pouting lips came to meet the filter with surprising gingerness, as though this one might contain a charge of dynamite. The lips then stopped short of the filter, protruded further in a kind of moist groping until the cigarette was drawn towards his face just enough to ensure a firm grasp. He then lit it with a lighter set to full flame.

He was wide-eyed rather than blinking when the

tobacco caught. If this one had a dynamite charge he wasn't about to miss the moment of ignition. He wanted the whole experience, just as he wanted the full effect of the nicotine, if it was indeed just an ordinary cigarette. I had not seen Clements smoke before.

For his first draw he maintained his pout as a way of keeping the maximum distance between the filter and his nacreous screw-in teeth. I thought once he had it going he would change his attitude, but as it turned out he smoked the entire cigarette in this manner.

'You want one?' he asked, making his offer very much as an afterthought.

'No, thanks,' I replied.

'You don't smoke?'

'No.'

'Very wise.'

He seemed to get a kick out of this exchange, which mystified me. Before putting the packet back in his pocket he tapped it with a fingernail where there was a customs import sticker. 'I got these from a policeman,' he said. 'Loot.'

'That's coppers for you, sir,' I said and glanced to the subject, indicating that he might offer a cigarette in that direction.

'Oh, he doesn't,' he said. Finally, he looked directly at the subject and spoke through a plume of blue smoke. 'What do you want to know?' he asked.

This took the subject by surprise. He was exhausted. He had been thoroughly grilled by the anti-terrorist mob. It occurred to me that this man wasn't what we all wanted. He wasn't young and idealistic. He wasn't a fanatic. He wasn't a suicide bomber. He had rationalised his mission and agreed to be exploited. He was a willing party to death and destruction on a grand scale because he was a messenger, a facilitator of change. He was a small, angry man burning to deliver a surprise. I thought of Mrs Espinosa's pathetic son and his horde of fire-works.

'Know . . . ?' he said, with a defiant canting of the head.

'About your situation,' Clements said.

'Who are you?'

'I'm a big spy.' The cadence was odd, as though there was a rich charge of irony that only he was privy to. Maybe that was why he was now getting a dis-proportionate amount of pleasure from his smoking. 'He's not so big,' he added, indicating me.

The subject looked at me with disgust – one grunt to another. But that in itself was him taking direction from Clements. Some connection had been made. 'You have heard all I have to say,' he said, addressing Clements but with his gaze lingering on me. 'You've been spying,' he said with a sneer.

Clements shrugged inoffensively. Took another pouty pull on his cigarette. 'How did it begin?' he asked. He endured a long silence before asking a second time, showing the same interest, the same patience.

No reply. Nor, it seemed, was one expected. Clements had come to look. To examine at close quarters. To satisfy himself that the pieces that were available to him were in place and that he was fully conversant with the detail. Perhaps it was also a lesson for me. It wasn't enough to analyse information if there was a face you could look at. You could probe.

'Right-o,' he said with a show of inattention, but with the same patience. He turned to me. 'He's an honest man. That's why he's saying nothing.'

I felt stupid nodding, but I nodded.

When the suspect spoke again – to complain about his treatment – he spoke as though he was simultaneously translating his own words. There seemed to be a slight delay at the end of each utterance while he appreciated the good job he was doing. The effect was a linguistic cockiness that instantly gave me the hump.

The solicitor took no notes.

'Ripe, isn't he?' I commented when we stepped away from the first of several armoured doors that would see us out.

'He smells of rotten sex,' Clements replied flatly. 'You don't think he's had sex recently, do you?'

The best face I could put on this question was that he was asking me because I was his field man and therefore should have a discerning nose for all things rotten. It was a rarefied kind of snobbery. The question, I knew, didn't require an answer.

We left by the front door, stepped out into the street and waited for Malcolm to drive the car around from the rear.

A rough-looking man came loping towards us. He was up on the balls of his feet but drained of energy. Vacant eyes, oblivious, easily toppled. A methadone case. He was clutching two golf clubs by their necks, pressed to his chest. The hold he had on the two irons suggested his life depended on his keeping them to himself.

Where was he going with his golf clubs in the dark? It was his grip on these golf sticks that made me feel sorry for him, and lacking in myself. I had to give myself a quick talking to.

He passed like a helium ghost, judging poorly the gap between us and the wall.

'What would you do with our friend inside?' Clements asked. He was watching our phantom golfer shamble down the street as though he might learn something about being more graceful in his clumsiness.

'He's a grunt. He doesn't have anything for us. I'd leave it to Special Branch.'

'PC plodders in furniture vans, some in the service would say.' It was a leading comment, I knew.

'Not me,' I said.

'Jolly good. But you're annoyed.'

I shrugged that off, but he was right. My blood was boiling.

I voiced thoughts I probably should have kept to myself. I wanted more of Clements's appraisal of the man. There was a lot I could learn from Clements's appraisal of men.

He responded with: 'His kind always thinks the push into the future has become even more acute, when really, Harry, they are jaded. The present used to be a plateau for them, and now it's a pinhead. One short shuffle. One big blast.'

I nodded sagely. I don't know why except perhaps to acknowledge a little extra depravity imposed upon the day.

'There's something in that for us,' he concluded vaguely. 'Something we can exploit.'

I continued to nod.

'Why do you ask my opinion of this man? What do you think I know?' Two disarming questions from a mentor designed to check the thoughtless nodding of his student.

'Research,' I heard myself utter. Which was scarcely an answer at all to either question.

'Never say you are doing research,' he said. He made it a mildly acidic reprimand. Almost indulgent. 'You wanted to sweat him,' he added.

'Not me.'

But I did. I wanted to break him. Clements was using his wily interrogator's skills on me now.

'It isn't all our fault,' he said.

'What?' I asked. Malcolm was following us in the car, dutifully crawling along by the kerb, trying to be inconspicuous while he stank up the vehicle. It wasn't right that there was so much stinking in a day.

'Life,' said Clements.

'Ahhh . . .'

'Doesn't mean to say we can't make it work, Harry.'

He wanted me to agree. That was part of making it work.

So, I agreed. I had been given corporate gas to

inhale and I inhaled it. 'What are you going to do with our friend?' I asked.

'Well,' he said, 'we could follow the example of the archbishop.'

'What's that?'

'There was an archbishop who had a monkey shot in the zoo for wanking too much.'

He broke me easily. I had to laugh. He didn't laugh at all, but his eyes where burning with complicity. He signalled to Malcolm to draw the car up and positioned himself awkwardly at the kerb.

Clements's physical clumsiness, his animal trait of being a poor judge of human movement, was something of a ruse. There was a skylight in his thinking that let in the light night and day. He wasted nothing when it came to processing information and character assessment. To deflect from the main order of business and thereby keep his counsel, he could make sugar cubes of any rogue thoughts and fire them out his nose for you to put in your tea.

We had learned nothing about bomb traffic that first visit, but Clements was taking a personal interest in the interrogation and had only just begun with our little rat friend.

CHAPTER 9

I was done with hiding. I was working again. The following day I went to the pile an hour early. Such was my enthusiasm for being, like Clements, one of life's great responders, everything seemed out of proportion. The furniture jumped when I came into the office. My colleagues were too big or too small. It was all a bit rubbery.

The temperature outside had crept up a few degrees then plummeted again. The heating system had broken down and this I took personally. I kicked the nice new radiator. That was me asserting that I now had a stake in the whole operation. The furniture jumped again and I went out to see if there was any heat on my floor.

There was none. The other floors were out too. It was an excuse for me to snoop. I like to snoop, even when I'm cranky and it's a rubbery day. Snooping was part of my job and needed to be practised on a regular basis if I wasn't to forget how good I was at it; if I was not to lose my nerve. Losing my nerve had become an issue with me. I think that's what had me hanging out of my caul with the tripes bursting from my wound as I made my rough landing in the old man's back garden.

Anyway, I didn't get far with my snooping. I met Clements on the corridor he called the Gallery.

Was I straying? he wanted to know. The man had to be a master snoop himself, so it must have been obvious to him what I was up to. Still, 'straying' was a curious word to use – even if it was an attempt at good humour – because I wasn't out of bounds.

'It's bloody freezing,' I said.

'Yes,' he said mildly. 'I know. Isn't it just.'

'What's the story with the heating?'

'The whole building is out.'

'When will it be fixed?'

'Oh, I'm sure they're working on it now.'

I must have sounded more than disgruntled. Being caught wandering the corridors just pointed up the limbo in which I found myself. I would have to be patient. I would make a map of this venture in thick crayon.

Being patient didn't blunt my desire to get warm. I grunted disapprovingly. Clements shrugged in a gesture of resignation. Being largely responsible for the security of the realm didn't include getting the heating to work.

The Gallery had benches with flat cushions which, in an earlier era, would have been stuffed with horse hair, but in ours doubtless doubled as flotation devices and makeshift bulletproof vests. He sat down on one of these. I was glad to do the same. Before, I'd been an understrapper, an un-official freelance grunt without a pension scheme.

Now, I was sitting in the Gallery with Mr Clements. I was hoping some of the monkeys in the pile were watching this – the chief taking time to talk to me on the cushions.

We were surrounded with the same acoustic deadener that lined the rest of the building. It helped to enforce an unnatural calm. You could get yourself a paper cone of chilled water and talk with colleagues here. You could select at random a bench on which to sit and brood if you didn't want to talk but the Gallery encouraged gossip, flirtation and flatulence. Some of these people wouldn't fart in their own offices.

There was nowhere else in the building where that randomness operated. Not even in the canteen. Being seen getting a talk from Clements in the canteen wouldn't have had the same effect.

I thought he was going to give me further information on our bomber; some instructions, perhaps, but instead he asked about my stab wound. There was a nice bit of hard-wearing carpet in the Gallery. I noticed it as I leaned forwards and switched focus from my clasped hands to the patch of carpet between my legs.

'That's all healed, Mr Clements,' I said. 'I'm a lucky man.'

He drew back his lips. 'We used to hire people for their skills and train them for attitude. Now, it's the reverse.' He rose to his feet. 'Always knew you had it both ways, Harry.'

And he was gone. I sat there for a moment, not knowing what I felt, then went and did some token snooping. I snooped my way back to my room. There was a stranger in it. He sprang up from behind the desk holding an electric fan heater.

'Ah ha,' he said.

I didn't like him *Ah-ha*ing me. The tone got my goat. He wasn't maintenance. He was wearing an expensive suit and shiny leather-soled office shoes. He had a flop-over haircut. I hate twits with flop-over haircuts. I would meet them every day now. I'd have to learn to indulge my prejudice in a sophisticated manner.

'Who the fuck are you?'

'Bryers.'

'Bryers . . . ?' I tried to sound incredulous.

'Charlie Bryers. This is for you, Harry,' he said, holding up the fan heater.

Now, there is something that gets my goat more than a flop-over public school twit. And that's a flop-over public school twit being familiar. He switched the heater to his other mitt so that he could shake my hand. It was a quick, hard handshake that made me feel I was being scanned for bad karma and robbed in the one move.

'Right, then,' I said, snatching the heater. 'I can take it from here.'

'Oh, but we have to see if it works,' he insisted. 'Mr Clements sent me down with this. Personally.'

'Did he? That's very kind of him. And very prompt.' Now, I was trying to sound sarcastic, but he chose to ignore the obvious.

'Everybody wants one. There aren't anything like enough to go round. You're lucky.'

It was an ancient thing I held in my hand. Made

of tin, not plastic. They must have brought these from the old premises. Thriftiness would always be a mandatory part of the service. Always seen as a sign of good character.

I handed it back to him. 'All right, then. See if it works.' Quite where this twerp belonged in the food chain I couldn't say, but if Clements had sent him and he was under orders to deliver heat I'd let him at it.

'I was just about to check when you came in,' he said with clipped forbearance.

'Very prompt, I must say,' I repeated as he crouched to plug in the heater behind my desk. His smart office shoes must have had steel inlays because they didn't crease to accommodate his position.

'There are no queues in Mr Clements's life,' he said as he threw the switch.

Nothing happened.

'Bugger,' he declared.

I perched my behind on the desk and looked around my little domain. I looked in the old cardboard box he had brought the heater in.

'What are you, then?' I asked. 'Special Operations?'

'Bugger. Bugger. Bugger.' Evidently, he ignored sarcasm in others as a matter of course. He stood up, produced a fancy penknife from his pocket, opened the screwdriver blade and proceeded to take apart the casing of the heater on my desk.

'Ah ha,' he said, as years of service fluff and dirt spilled out. 'Bloody thing is clogged. Look at that.' He pulled great tufts from the fan wheel and blades. He took out a mat of dirt from the grille behind the element. He was meticulous. He might as well have been looking for a micro bug.

And, maybe he was.

'I hope this is going to work,' I said. 'I'm bloody freezing up here.'

'There's bound to be a trip button on this model,' he mumbled to himself.

'Oh good,' I barked.

'Leave it to me, Harry,' he said with a flick of his flop-over.

I did leave it to him and I shouldn't have. I should have turfed him out on his pink little ear. He got the heater going, then he saw that my computer screen was dark. He seemed to read this as a bad omen. A concrete manifestation of knowledge in arrears. 'Isn't it working?' he asked with a brittle politeness.

Being a fully-fledged member of the flock, I made no attempt to conceal my annoyance, but that didn't bother him. He was on a secret mission. 'I don't know,' I said. There was nothing wrong with it but I didn't mind trading on his keen sense of propriety. He found it hard to take in my indifference, but covered well.

'There's been a few problems,' he said, moving into position, making ready for a diagnosis.

'Really?'

'Little gremlins. Nothing to do with security, just traffic. None of my business, but I could take a look for you.'

'Another time, maybe.'

'You're thinking you can always ring IT. Well, can

I just say my experience is that IT people, as a rule, don't answer the telephone.'

'All right, then,' I said.

'I'm not really supposed to,' he said with relish as he switched the computer on. 'Let's see if they've set you up properly. It all should be in order, but . . .'

'Yes. I know.'

'Ah – they have. You're in business.'

'Don't I need a password?'

'For your terminal, yes. As you'd have on your own computer at home.' He couldn't believe he had a computer simpleton on his hands. He was hugely entertained. I thought I'd help him along.

'I don't have one at home.'

He flushed with delight. 'You don't? Well . . . never mind. You put your own little password on here – just to stop people like me from prying.'

'Right. I will.'

'If you paid a visit to IT you might be able to cadge a laptop. If you were clever about it. You could take that home with you. They've bundles of them downstairs – though they won't admit it, of course.'

'Thank you. I'll remember that.'

I was eager to get him out. We were standing in the doorway now. His lighthouse eyes locked on to a beanpole man in a tailored suit passing in the corridor.

'You know him?' he asked out the side of his mouth.

I recognised him as Baldwin, the man from Internal Security Clements had introduced me to in the underground garage, but I shook my head. Until Bryers informed me, everybody in the pile except me knew that Baldwin was heading the internal inquiry into the activities of the latest whistle-blower. One Gordon G. had blabbed to the press about pre-emptive action by the firm; that is to say, plans to assassinate rogue political figures, sponsors and their agents of terrorism. He had taken files, only a few of which he had shown to date. There was other material pertaining to unacceptable behaviour by the firm – events that had already taken place. Nobody would say what behaviour this was. I wasn't in the mood for office games with Bryers. I had indulged him enough already.

'We call him "The Knight",' he said, his eyes following Baldwin as he moved away and turned into an adjoining corridor.

How many concentric circles in personnel did 'we' embrace? 'Really?' I said. 'How interesting.'

He wasn't to be put off. 'We call him that because of his moving forwards then sideways.'

'As in chess?' I said with an insincere brightness. I didn't believe anybody else called Baldwin the Knight. Bryers had made it up just to see if it would travel. To see if I would pass it on.

'As in chess,' he repeated smoothly. 'Lethal right-angle turns. Dickie Baldwin. Deputy in charge of the security mob.'

'We don't want him coming back round that corner, do we?'

He gave a shrill, nervous laugh and looked me up and down. I was his kind of sparring mate. I could tell. I would have to learn to keep my mouth firmly shut.

'You are so right,' he said, beaming. 'We do not.'

Bryers stepped out into the corridor, lingered a moment as if he might hear some tell-tale noise from around the corner. His reptile lids which, until now, had covered the upper third of the pupils, lifted a third as much again, an act designed to convey that he was highly intelligent and not in a dull way. Valiant against all disaster. With the eye-widening exercise I could have sworn his contact lenses rolled around the back of his eyeballs momentarily. He stood frozen like a statue, inviting my scrutiny.

I wanted to annoy him. 'You think we should follow him?' I asked.

That didn't go down well. I had scoffed at his little piece of opera. Suddenly, I was a disappointment. I'd failed to learn a lesson here, though I couldn't think what that lesson might be.

He put his hand out for me to shake just in case I didn't recognise that our encounter had ended. This was altogether a slower handshake than the one he greeted me with. I noticed now that his hand was oily. Not mechanics' oil. Human, on the slimy end of the spectrum. He left abruptly and made his way to the lift.

I didn't give Charlie Bryers or Dickie Baldwin much thought. I had more practical concerns at that point. My new-found enthusiasm and commitment notwithstanding, could I get somebody else to do any routine computer work that came my way? I was hoping I could keep my computer time to an absolute minimum. I get easily confused when I'm inside a computer. This was not good for any person looking for advancement in the security services.

Who did I think I was fooling? My computer in-eptitude was immediately apparent even to the lowliest apparatchik. No amount of tutoring would make me anything other than barely competent. Clements, I told myself, had the good sense to keep me out of the office and in the field with this new office job he had given me.

If I was going to be out most of the time, averting wrongful acts, I had better make sure my e-mail and messaging service was operative, I decided. So, for the first time, I sat down properly at my desk – that is to say, at right angles and with my feet under the top – and stared at my computer screen. I didn't think about the loyalty, presence of mind in a crisis and field skills that finally had brought about my induction. I thought about Juno.

Now that you're safe and sound in the bosom of MI5, she whispered out of nowhere, why don't you go and screw little Ruthy, wife of your dear dead friend, Alfie?

I'm otherwise engaged.

CHAPTER 10

Juno wouldn't let me sleep. She kept making mock love noise with Jack Bradley. My mouth was dry. My muscles were aching from prolonged contraction. I let out an involuntary wail that I recognised as the spiritual edge of an all-embracing panic.

I got up and paced the room. Should I throw on my clothes and tramp the streets? It was windy out and my legs were shaky. I could go to some all night cafeteria. Was it my imagination or was somebody in this building actually tightening screws into sheet metal or dry wood?

My floor pacing got faster, more erratic. I went to the sink and drank down great gulps of water. I was swallowing air at the same time instead of taking even breaths. I could have drowned. This was no way for a good spy to behave.

You've got to speak now, Harry, I thought. Make it clear. What are you afraid of? What do you need to fix? SPEAK IT OUT. That's the right kind of madness.

It was, I decided, incredible that I'd secured the job of personal assistant to Clements. That I was party to his works. Agent in the thwarting of future bombers. But, I wasn't in good shape. That was my secret, and it was clawing to get out.

'I'm not feeling well, you know,' I said aloud.

Yes, I know, said the voice.

'I'm not well here – in the heart.'

I understand.

I didn't expect the prompt response. I was glad of it when it came.

Old news, Harry.

'Juno. Juno.'

Juno did not respond, but I couldn't get her out of my head. Her and Bradley.

There is a purpose in this sadness, the voice said. Think about your old man dying. Think about Alfie. Think about screwing his wife. Think about your new job. Don't think about Juno.

Nothing the voice said assuaged my fear, except that the voice was kind and that surprised me.

So, I spoke up about my secret. My loss of nerve. My fear of not being good enough in the crucial moment; of being too slow or too late. The fear of hesitation that might have me on the wrong side of humane when some bastard wanted to damage me or somebody close to me. The fear of betrayal.

All my fears were old fears. I had got stuck on that.

The jumpiness hadn't left when I went to the office. As part of my private programme of redemption I rang my brother, Peter. I wanted to make peace with him. Things had happened between us in the past – I had brought him trouble and he hadn't forgiven me for this. Now, I wanted his forgiveness.

The conversation didn't go well. I told him I had been promoted. That set him off. I didn't give a damn about him or his family. I don't contact him for a year or more then I ring him to tell him I've got promotion in my sordid little job. I was selfish, reckless and uncaring.

These were old jibes but I was struck by the freshness of his rage. I could take this kind of abuse from a brother but I chose not to. I put down the phone. My altogether-far-too-responsible brother was losing the run of himself. He was trouble.

Selfish, yes. Uncaring, no. And certainly not reckless.

I shouldn't have rung him. And, as it would turn out, I shouldn't have put the phone down.

Clements had somebody he wanted me to meet. This introduction took place in my poky office. They got the two chairs while I stood like an eejit in front of the computer.

'We want to tell Harry about you, don't we?' Clements said.

'Oh yes,' Trevor replied boldly. Trevor was a dandified, slightly ripe individual. He took in my features as he might take in picture food in the window of a Japanese restaurant. I took an instant dislike to him. I thought it would be useful to be a bit testy, just to tease him out.

'Let me guess,' I said, 'you're in the antique trade.'

'Very perceptive of you,' he replied in a jolly tone, 'but no. I have a brother in the antique trade, looks a lot like me. Maybe you met him.'

'Maybe.'

He was bursting out of his stylish, hard-worn clothes. He caught me clocking the freshly whitened old-fashioned tennis shoes which he wore with his suit. 'Yes, I know,' he said with an expansive swoon. 'Bit of an accident.'

I couldn't imagine what that might mean. 'I was just going to remark on how white and clean they are.'

He gave a pained smile.

'He does have a brother in antiques,' Clements volunteered. Glad to see me breaking the ice but properly anxious about where I was going. 'The brother is a fence and Trevor here was a thief. You were a thief, weren't you, Trevor?'

The pained smile lingered. 'I was in supply and demand.'

'A thief?' I exclaimed with mock surprise.

'I was in procurement.' Now, he was being extra coy. I didn't like that at all. I fucking hate parlour games. 'Quality stuff. I lifted to order. That way there was no confusion. There are short-term profits in confusion, but really, it's never the way to proceed.'

'He's finished with that, as such, haven't you, Trevor?' Christ. Now Clements was being coy.

'I have, sir.'

'But you could steal for us – if asked?'

'I could, of course, sir.'

The 'sirs' didn't sit well either. Trevor was too much the aristocratic lounge lizard for them to ring true.

'You should steal yourself a pair of shoes,' I suggested.

'I will, Harry.'

'Are you lucky?' I asked.

'Lucky?'

'Have you ever been caught?'

'Never.'

I didn't believe his whipped dog act. The eyes were convincing, but the feet were not. They were too sure of themselves, tapping each other on the ends of his outstretched legs. He was clever in a thick sort of way. That meant — in a blunt, animal way — he was dangerous.

Another stabber, I thought. No hesitation. Or, a throat cutter. You wouldn't see it coming. I kept my eyes on him. I didn't blink. He would pick up on that. No doubt he thought he was inviting my disdain with his nervy evasiveness. He would be very pleased and just a little less on his guard. The mistake these monkeys make is that they think you've never met anyone like them before. That's where the thickness shows.

The only difference between this one and others I had encountered was that he had a marcel wave in his hair.

The glass was cracked on his lumpy gold watch. He had an elastic band around one wrist and wore a faded green button-down collar shirt the collar wings of which were unbuttoned. His skin was over-scrubbed. His suit jacket was too long. I was sure the flaps were concealing spermy trousers. Definitely a killer.

'You'll be working together,' Clements announced. 'Trevor is eager to earn his stripes.'

I gave him a big smile. I could see Trevor stepping out from some filthy doorway in his tennis shoes late one night and approaching with the low-slung run of an attacking Alsatian.

An awkward silence followed. Clements looked to each of us in turn. 'You two want to say something to one another?' he said.

It was an unexpected, eccentric challenge.

'Eh . . . well . . .' I stuttered.

'You want to have a convesation?' The repeated challenge was just as disconcerting.

'Yes,' my unsavoury colleague blurted out confidently, if a little late. He had decided this was a trick question. A test. I could tell by the blank expression on his face, however, that he had not decided what kind of test.

There was silence. I looked to him directly. He had come out with the yes answer. It was up to him to lead. I certainly had nothing more to say to him, and now I was intrigued by Clements's out-of-character schoolteacher's tone, not to say appalled at the prospect of Trevor being my new apprentice.

Clements continued to look impatiently from one of us to the other, showing no sign of moving in any direction. 'You want me to give you a topic?' he asked.

We both laughed nervously. Some language gadget that was meant to be activated had failed.

Perhaps this was a ploy after all. Clements injecting a strange updraft designed to put a sharp check on gossip, real and imagined?

'Eh . . . well . . .' I repeated, this time without the stutter.

'Nice talking, Harry,' Trevor said, just to jolly things along.

Was it nice to talk? We hadn't said much.

'Is that the bloody time?' he said, glancing at his lumpy watch. He turned with the slightest of nods and left the room. Evidently, he didn't have to excuse himself from Clements's company. This added to my paranoia. I wanted to ask Clements why he was putting this thug at my back, but I knew better. 'Trevor stinks,' I said. 'Not like our bomber friend, but he does smell.'

Clements nodded. 'You would think vanity and cleanliness go together, wouldn't you?' He told me that under no circumstances was I to bring the man into his office.

The day had hardly begun and I needed to lie down.

It was a happy coincidence that, for security reasons, all dealings with Trevor were to be conducted informally. Ostensibly, Trevor had no official status – he had my old job of understrapper, and he was working to me.

Ostensibly.

My gut tightened further. As it turned out, it wouldn't be long before Trevor performed his first good deed.

CHAPTER 11

Strength before happiness. I should have gone directly to Juno to have it out with her, but I wasn't ready yet. So, instead, I went to 'screw little Ruthy'. I had it in my head that my feeling guilty was better than my giving in to the hurt and the rage. That way around there was clarity. The well-sprung argument of a true spy, wouldn't you say, Mr Clements?

I went with Ruth to her suburban house in Carshalton to help her with packing. We were there just a few minutes and had done nothing when I pinned her hands to the back of the door and reminded her that our Alfie had been gone a long stretch now. 'Don't let him break your heart again,' I said. I couldn't believe my own dubiousness, nor the ease with which it cradled my desires.

Though the tips of her fingers came down gently on mine, she would not speak. Though our fingers then intertwined, she looked away.

'Be brave, Ruth,' I said. 'There, you see, you're crying because it's hard to be brave.'

I must have thought it was my only way through to her. My own desperation was acute, but she didn't see it, I was sure, beyond my whispered words. In spite of myself, here was a chance at love – that was my feverish assessment. I couldn't see why Ruth would have such feeling for me, in spite of our intimacy.

The numbness, I promised blindly, would go away. I didn't say that I meant my own as well as hers.

We went upstairs and I pushed into her among her neat piles of clothes and her cardboard boxes of household goods. We would do this again and again, I thought, but we did it now as though it would be the last time. We were almost grateful for the pervasive urgency and the wistful sadness that brought its own kind of sweetness.

The room might have been full of detractors standing around with tea cups filled with whiskey. We were able to ignore them. We were able to ride them out.

Alfie had told me his wife had grown up in a house where the taps dripped from years of being shut off too tightly. She was more susceptible to infection, he said, because her mother was constantly disinfecting every utensil, every surface. Ruth had burned out the motor on several of her mother's hoovers just to please her mother's zeal for hoovering, and here she was in her friend's kip of a flat ramming as hard as me without protection, surrounded perhaps by crook-fingered whiskey drinkers.

I saw in Ruth's face an exhaustion which I could not distinguish from the exhaustion that comes with the struggle to comprehend acts of great cruelty.

That drove me in harder still. In spite of myself I wanted to make her love me. Not in place of Alfie, but from this moment; from no other.

And suddenly, my thrusting was part of a chant of desire, a prayer that I could not make lighter than the ether. It would not stay airborne. It would not travel. It settled in ribbons around us.

There were shrieks from children down in the street.

'Can I do running?' a child cried.

'Yes, you can do running,' came the adult reply.

And there was running.

The Missing Person file on Alfie had been closed and a murder investigation launched. There would never again be any mention of his crooked dealings. There would only be reference to what I was sure would be the fruitless quest for his killers.

She didn't say that she wanted me to stay the night. Nor did she send me away. She slept heavily, with only the occasional whimper. I didn't sleep at all. I jumped out of the bed when it began to rain thunderously. From the bedroom window I saw a dozen large, flaccid drops make a puddle in an instant. For a few minutes the smell of dry tarmacadam getting soaked was as pungent as freshly cut grass. Then, as suddenly as it began, it was over and the smell was gone. The water ran down the drains in double quick time and I wept for my lost friend.

In the morning I accompanied Ruth to the funeral home where we stood by the sealed box. She wanted me to stay with her in the room. She held my arm. She wanted to comfort me.

★   ★   ★

Clements was going to sweat the bomber in his own sweet way. He didn't care that this would cause resentment among Special Branch, the anti-terrorist mob and the firm's inquisitors. This time I would drive him to Paddington. There would be no Malcolm.

I meet Bryers in the lift on the way to the car pool.

'You're not going to believe this,' he said. He liked theatre. Pouting indignantly, centre stage. Very much larger than life, calling to order a magnificent shambles. A true flâneur, if only he was afforded the time. If only he didn't have to sort out the mess. I really wasn't in the mood.

'What?'

'It's outrageous . . .'

'What?'

'I go to the canteen for a cup of tea . . .'

'And?'

'And a biscuit.'

'And – WHAT?'

'I have to – *pay* for the biscuit.'

I left a silence. He liked that. I think he thought I was in the same play and was as outraged as he. Then my jaded expression must have registered.

'We've never had to pay for a biscuit,' he said. His tone seemed to suggest that I was the one who had charged him.

'Really?' I said. 'And how much do they want for a biscuit?'

'That's not the point, is it?'

I shrugged. I had mistaken his question for a rhetorical remark. I must have been distracted by the hunt for terrorists with weapons of mass destruction.

'Is it?' he demanded.

I changed my expression to a wince and gave another shrug. 'You're capable,' I said. 'I'm sure you can swipe a biscuit or two.'

He could, but that wasn't the point either. He could see I wasn't a player after all. But that was a challenge. He delighted in awkward challenges. He liked a bit of cheek. Insolent young pup was a compliment he bestowed on favourites, whatever their age.

I wasn't so blessed that day.

'Look,' I said, purely to make mischief, 'if *you* can't do anything about them charging for biscuits, nobody can.' I would have to learn that any kind of flattery, save the most puerile and sentimental, was greeted with rank suspicion by this man, whatever the desired effect.

'That is not the point,' he repeated. Instead of placing heavy emphasis on the *not* he lightly slid across the top of the word, a breathy reminder of a higher moral plane.

You see, this was the kind of eccentric conversation I feared I would be party to on a daily basis if I took a desk job with the firm. This kind of nonsense would quickly dull my brain and would have me lose perspective and, eventually, see me behave in this manner myself. 'Fuck them,' I said, 'we'll bring in our own biscuits.'

He screwed up his eyes and shifted his weight. 'Somebody told me you were Irish. Is that right?'

'Every other day.'

'What?'

'Half.'

He nodded, not at all surprised by his grasp of modes of human behaviour. 'Quick with that sort of thing,' he said. He managed to be patronising, approving and slightly mysterious all at once. The implication was that if nobody else could give me a brief he would find a use for me.

There was a long silence between us in the car on the way to Paddington. Not an awkward silence. More one of expectation on my part. An anxiety born of an eagerness to make good.

Clements came up out of a deep, thoughtful hole. 'That this house will in no circumstances fight for its king and country,' he put out formally.

'Sorry, sir?'

'Motion.'

'Yes . . . ?'

'Discuss.'

I scrambled to get an angle. This was some kind of test. I wanted to impress. I tried to buy a little time to think. '*King and country* . . . when was this, Mr Clements?'

'Oxford Union. 1933. Does that matter?'

'Well, it's democracy in action, isn't it? It's healthy somebody proposes the like from time to time.'

'Good answer.'

I couldn't tell if he was mocking me. 'And the result?' I asked.

'What?'

'The result of the debate, Mr Clements?'

'The motion carried.'

'Really?' I left a silence then blurted out – 'I want to do well. I want to learn properly. I could run agents.'

'I know that, Harry.'

Clements sat a long time with his pet bomber. Neither man spoke. When Clements abruptly got up to leave the subject rose to his feet, apparently before he quite realised what he was doing.

Later that evening I undertook some compulsive action of my own. I wanted to finish with more of the past so I bought a shovel in a hardware shop and I went to Ruth's house and began to dig in the back garden. It was one of those short trench shovels that keeps you close to the point of contact with the earth. It made for a short swing with the dirt over the shoulder.

I set to digging for Alfie's unlisted treasure. Digging for Ruth. I understand now that in her eyes my frenzied action was inordinately strange, even frightening. She saw I wasn't drunk, that this was a bizarre act of grieving, or a kind of sickness. She saw a man who had been too long hiding in the sun. The solitary and uncompromising Harry finally unhinged by the death of his friend, but really, I just wanted to be free of the guilt. Had you told me I was having a breakdown, I would have laughed. Something slow and slimy and hostile was wrapping itself around that deserted house in Carshalton and I was determined to finish my digging. In my head I wasn't going any faster than a starving cowboy in the desert eating his saddle.

I dug holes everywhere and found nothing. I got blisters on my hands that burst and bled. A neighbour must have rung Ruth. She embraced me now in something like the Heimlich manoeuvre, but executed from the front. It calmed me instantly. It brought on the Fielding apnoea.

Things were going right, I was thinking without drawing breath. I hadn't found anything in the garden, but I had heard Alfie telling me he'd arrived safely on the other side of oblivion. I could now measure the distance in passage of time to the next world. I could count from the day Alfie was killed to this point of madness in his back garden. It had taken him this long to get there, see the big picture and make his report. Thank you, Alfie.

I looked around at what I had done. At my mad-dog landscape. At the hacked roots and the wet worms. My madness was already passing, but I knew that there was no future for Ruth and me together. I wanted to howl and rant at this bitter wisdom, but my lungs were locked.

'Oh, Ruth,' I whispered with the air that remained in my throat.

'Shhh, Harry,' she said, stepping back a quarter pace but still maintaining the embrace. She kept full eye contact, in spite or because of her alarm, I couldn't tell which. 'Come away. There's nothing here.'

'No,' I admitted. 'There isn't.'

'Put that down. Just leave it there.'

I let go of the shovel. She squeezed both my hands. For the first time I felt the pain of burst blisters and the stickiness of my quick-drying blood.

She took me into the kitchen and ran the cold tap. That was when the persistent tattoo on a car horn began. We ignored it at first, but then I went to investigate. Trevor had come to perform his good deed.

He wound down his window and shouted to me. 'Harry,' he said, 'you'll need a lift.'

How long had he been there? He had followed me here, of course. He was going to give me a lift wherever I wanted to go, then he was going to report to Clements.

CHAPTER 12

A thing can be disappointing and you want to move on quickly, but when somebody tells me they're disappointed my palms begin to itch and I get a sour taste in my mouth.

Bryers came to me before I went to Clements. He said Clements would be disappointed that I was finding it difficult to settle in, as he put it. That bollix, Trevor, had used the same phrase. It was his way of associating himself with middle management. 'They'll be disappointed,' he had said. Everybody got jittery when an agent showed signs of a nervous breakdown, he added piously.

Being disappointed – it's a phoney state.

'I'm disappointed,' they say, but they aren't. Not really. They are indulging themselves at your expense, and they want to make it last. It doesn't get more phoney than when they express disappointment in you. That's when they need a smack on the head without warning. Without explanation. If violence isn't appropriate all I can do is scratch my palms and scrape my tongue on my top front teeth, and that's disappointing. It has me looking for the door and suddenly I'm on my feet and I'm on my way.

Disappointment of another kind was part of the firm's coded language. This also had me looking for the door. Whatever the specifications, I knew that in this line of work the agent was required to assume dirty dealing, if not outright treachery on the part of others. Assume as much in each instance until our controller cautioned that we were behaving like the scientist who has made the mistake of falling in love with his own theory. Then, we could be disappointed with impunity. I'd have to tell Clements I was very fucking disappointed Trevor's brief was to spy on me.

'And by the way,' said Bryers, delighted to be witness to more of my troubles, 'your brother called.'

'He called?'

'Yes. Called to the premises. Created a scene.'

It was bad enough that he should visit. Worse that there should have been any kind of a scene. 'What are you talking about?'

'He wanted to see you. When he was told you weren't available he created a scene.'

'A scene? What kind of a scene?'

'He had a rant, I'm told. We don't normally have our brother calling to the premises, do we?'

He was rubbing my nose in it now. I couldn't bear his supercilious sneering. His use of the royal 'we'.

'No, we don't,' I yawped.

'He's been round twice in the one day, apparently.'

'What did he want?'

'Christ, man, I don't answer the door. Ask the porter.'

Clements didn't profess disappointment when I

went to see him. He didn't look at the plasters on my hands. Instead, he instructed me to take a little time out. I was getting unofficial sick leave from my unofficial post. If I was needed urgently Clements would call me in. There was that patience again. That time-making. He had his coat on. He was going to sit with his bomber.

You get yourself set up in a nice flat – that was his line. If I was stuck for the deposit he would see me right. Get somewhere decent, he advised. Comfort was important, and it needed to be a place where I could entertain. He wanted to build my self-image, to provide for the idea of an instantly recognisable independence that was inseparable from a set of instantly recognisable responsibilities.

'What about your brother, Harry?' he asked.

'Yes, sir. I know. He called here. Upset about something. I'll have to talk to him.' That sounded rich coming from me, the state I was in. God almighty, I had it all straight in my head, my passage to a new and secure existence with the firm, and now it was all unravelling.

'Is he in trouble?'

'I don't know, Mr Clements. We don't see much of each other.'

'If he's in trouble you must help him.'

'Yes, sir.'

Public service and private actions drew on the same moral tenets. That was another of Clements's lines. A man who didn't invest in his family didn't invest in the greater political good. I was to take time with my family. To soothe my nerves. To reconnect with ordinary life. Both my family and the firm were lucky to have me. He wanted me to know that. He was looking after me on that basis. He wanted me to know that, too.

Another fact. I was more sick than I'd thought. I was Clements's loyal tower of jelly. But he saw my worth. I was sure of it. He saw I would make good.

What the fuck did my brother want? I feared the humdrum trouble he might bring. I was being groomed to hunt terrorists. I didn't want his problems, whatever they were. I feared he would have me fatally distracted, looking out for some small ruinous act of undoing.

So I was being brave when I rang him again. 'What the fuck do you want, Peter, calling to my place of work?' I asked, bravely.

Aunt Kate had rung him, he told me – an exceptional occurrence in itself – because she hadn't been able to raise me. She was ill. She hadn't taken the death of our father well. Her faltering spirit and her ailments, in part at least, could be attributed to that event. It was the first instance I could recall since childhood where she had asked Peter or myself to come to her.

It wasn't like Peter to create a scene over an ailing relative. I smelled a rat. I wanted to tell him I was busy hunting terrorists and bugging friendly politicians and diplomats – that would get his goat – but I resisted. Resisted because I cared about Kate.

He ranted on about not being able to contact me. It had fallen to him to mount a mercy mission.

So I rang Kate. She deflected talk about herself, just as I planned to do regarding myself. She spoke about her latest beau, who was a gardener. She would only refer to him as the Gardener. She wouldn't even tell me what kind of garden this man worked. Whether he worked one large domain or a string of modest suburban plots. She did, however, tell me that the Gardener had had a heart attack.

'It just goes to show,' she added with heavy significance, 'gardens aren't always the answer.'

The answer to what? To being old. To staying able and fit, in body and mind.

What could I say? I could only agree.

'He was down on his knees,' she said, 'he has one of those little kneeling stool things, and he's digging away when he gets the belt.' I heard her thump her breast with a fist made of her delicate, bony fingers.

'Really? That's unfortunate.'

'Digging away with his little trowel and he gets this terrible belt.' She gave a second thump. She didn't think you could over-emphasise a thing like this.

'I suppose it's good that he wasn't behind the wheel of a car,' I said, trying to catch the mood.

'On his knees, happily digging away, and probably whistling to himself.'

'And where is he now?' I asked with some trepidation.

'Back in the garden. He's really quite healthy for his age. It's just . . .' her voice trailed off '. . . you never know.'

'Do you see him often?'

'When it suits me,' she replied. The voice was back

very quickly, and more assertive than before. 'He's not the usual sort for a gardener. He's only quiet when it suits him. He can speak on any subject. You want to watch those ones. But *you* know that, don't you?' She changed gear. 'Now look, Harold,' she said, 'if I go peculiar or I have a stroke there's to be no miracle juice. No mysterious treatments.'

I gave a polite chuckle, but she was being serious. Serious about the Gardener, and about her becoming incapacitated. 'Right,' I said. 'I understand.'

'Good boy. I knew you would.' She didn't seem to think I was cracking up. 'They have me on the waffen,' she said, mispronouncing the blood-thinning drug they were now administering to her on regular visits to the local hospital out-patients' unit. 'That's quite enough.' But it wasn't. She added: 'The Gardener tells me he uses the same stuff to poison rats. Only, a stronger dose.'

'The rats haven't a chance with that stuff,' I said. She liked that.

'Remember, Harold,' she said, with even weightier significance, 'I'm a member of the Hemlock Society.' Which she was not.

'Yes, Kate,' I replied, trying to match her weightiness. 'I know.'

She wasn't a complainer. She wasn't looking for sympathy. She liked the idea of poison keeping her alive and wanted to share it with her favourite nephew. She had instructed me years before that when she died I was to ensure that she was cremated. She wanted me to arrange for a slender hand in a red satin elbow-length glove to come out from behind the oven curtain to wave goodbye just after she had been moved through on the conveyor. I had agreed to this request. This was all real to me. More real to me than my brother throwing a tantrum in the entrance hall of the MI5 building. It was an anchor. I drew her out further.

The Gardener, she told me, had a good head of hair but a bad carriage, visited irregularly and without warning. 'He could show up at any time,' she said. 'Loping up the path, looking very shifty for a man of his age.'

She wasn't apologising for him, she insisted. She was preparing us for interruptions if ever we were to visit her again. She was willing to tell me more. She wanted to keep me talking. It was a bonus that I hadn't met him.

'*You'd* know he wasn't shifty, dear, being a spy,' she said to me in an apologetic aside.

Clements was happy to sanction the few days for me provided I could be contacted at all times. I took it that this was his way of saying I was still gainfully employed by the firm. My services to his office could be done without while I put my house in order.

I was concerned about my aunt and happy to be seeing her again, but I was also ready to pounce at the first show of self-righteousness from my brother. I observed him entering the terminal building at Heathrow with a hauty peacock strut. What you need, Peter, when taking the high moral ground with me, is a fuse this length. It gives you enough time to – bang.

He was my brother. He knew what he was dealing with. Other people's failings are attractive, bar those of a sibling or parent.

For the first time I felt the need to comment on the fact that Peter's hair was really quite grey. It resembled the black and grey stuffing of a quality mattress. I made a mental note to tell him as much at another, more inopportune time. Perhaps when I took him to task over his calling to the pile and creating a scene.

'I'm looking forward to seeing Kate,' I said to him with a poke. We were sitting side by side in the concourse. He was twitching while he watched passengers scan the magazine racks in WH Smith. I was counting bombers.

'So am I,' he replied indignantly. 'She deserves better than to be sick and on her own.'

The sentiment rang hollow. There was more twitching. That would have been a good moment to bring up the greying hair and his idiot behaviour, but our flight was called. I could take some satisfaction in knowing that when I did use the jibe, I wouldn't have to admit that, actually, the combination of black and grey suited him. It went with his sense of authority which, for some reason, had been lacking when it came to the issue of our father, Cecil, and the home.

Kate came to her front window and stood by the two-handled vase she had let Peter and me drink lemonade out of when we were children. She had heard the car pulling up outside. From her demeanour I wasn't sure that she could see us clearly, but she wanted to be seen at her window welcoming her two nephews.

She gave a delicate wave as we came through the gate to which we responded enthusiastically. I noted the time it took her to reach the hall door.

'Here they are,' she announced, though there was nobody else in the house. She looked us both up and down as if we had turned up in response to a 'Smart Boy Wanted' ad in the evening papers.

'Well look at you, Aunt Kate,' I said and reached to embrace her.

'You expected to see me on the flat of my back,' she said. 'I know that. You can't fool me.'

For the first year in a very long time she had not taken the ferry to Liverpool for the Grand National at Aintree. She was wearing the glasses she had always protested were enemies. She had them on a slender gold chain with little leather lasso knots on the arms.

The glasses got in the way of her kissing me and Peter on the cheek. She had put on powder tan and cherry-red lipstick. She wouldn't have answered the door without full make-up on.

'Aunt Kate,' Peter said formally, but with warmth, 'it is so good to see you. How are you feeling?'

'Now,' she said, 'here's a news flash – I'm a long way from being a corpse.'

She was still alert, still engaged by life, but clearly it was getting harder for her. Peter's concern was more than justified. This bout of illness had knocked her for six. Though she had taken hold of me to lead the way into the living room it was as if a child had put her hand in mine. Her shoulder blades were getting progressively further apart; her back more rounded. The poise of a young, curvaceous woman in fashionable shoes had finally given way to the stiffness and primitive balance of old age.

The house smelled of dead flowers and furniture polish. In the living room we couldn't see much of the mad vine-patterned wallpaper for the framed photographs and paintings. It was more cluttered than I remembered from my last visit. She had taken stuff down from the attic; stuff that hadn't been displayed for thirty years or more.

Whatever she thought was worth displaying was out. She didn't know who some of the people in the photographs were. Their identities had been lost in time.

Pride of place went to the photograph of her and my mother in their swimsuits in 1956. They were jumping in the air, delighting in their outrageous behaviour. I knew it well. My father had taken it. His framed copy was one of the few things I had taken for myself from his mantelpiece when it was time to clear out his house.

'We're going to be looking after you for a few days,' Peter assured her nervously as he moved around to settle her in an armchair.

'No you're not,' she replied.

'Ah, we are,' I confirmed. 'And we're out for a good time, aren't we, Peter?'

He nodded awkwardly. 'Of course we are.'

'The plans other people have for you,' Kate declared as a resolute rebuke. She sank into the chair and was already feeling better than she had a minute earlier. 'Look,' she said, pointing to a corner of the worn Persian rug that Peter had inadvertently flipped up, 'you'll trip on that.'

And he nearly did.

CHAPTER 13

I didn't come to the firm via public school and Oxbridge. Now, those people wanted to belong to the firm, but I wanted it more. That compounded my failure of nerve and made a dull madness of it. Clements knew that I would need to be clear of all competing pressures if I was to be of any use and that would involve my being eternally grateful.

That evening, while I brooded over my fate instead of paying attention to competing pressures, Kate took my brother and me to her local pub.

'This place has changed hands,' she said. It didn't sound as though she was impressed. 'It happened last Monday. Needless to say, it was packed. Everybody in for their free drink.'

'You were there?'

'I was.'

'You got your free drink?'

'"What are you having, Kate?" he says to me. He's a smart one, the new owner, but he doesn't fool me.'

'No. I'm sure he doesn't. What's his game, then?'

'He goes to one party, introduces himself, offers them their drink on the house. Then he peers across at somebody else and he says "Now, I know that person. Who's this she is?" And they say it's Kate. And he comes over to me and pretends he knows me. 'What are you having, Kate?' And all around the pub he goes, doing the same thing.'

'Well,' I said, 'I suppose there are worse approaches.'

'He doesn't need to pretend, lovey. Not with me.'

She still had her cheeky smile. She quite fancied the new owner, she seemed to be saying, but he had botched his opportunity with her.

'I blame the Americans,' she said, 'with their high pressure techniques.'

'Really?'

'I do.' There was a brief pause. 'Still,' she mused, 'I like Americans.'

The following day we hired a car. Aunt Kate was ill but she still had her vanity. She put on more lipstick and insisted she sit in the front passenger seat with the window wound down two-thirds. She tied a scarf tightly to her head. She was calling it a picnic in spite of the fact that the only provisions we brought were a large tartan flask filled with tea, and her hip flask filled with Jameson. The hip flask always came with her to the races. She hadn't been to the local races either for some time.

The tension was hopping off Peter. It was probably hopping off me, too. I was concentrating hard to make this visit a success in as short a time as possible, but some things you can't rush. You can't force the pace.

Kate was glad to have another occasion to make use

of her silver flask. Both flasks were in a shopping bag, the dirty thing that she wouldn't surrender. The bag with her transistor radio in it. The transistor with batteries she claimed she bought in sex shops because, she said, they were the cheapest outlets for batteries.

I could see Peter choking on this piece of light smut. I could see him buying a new shopping bag and sending it to Kate and it going on the mountain of other unused bags.

The plan was that we would drive out of the city and up into the Wicklow mountains for the air and for our phantom picnic, then eat in a hotel.

I drove. Kate directed me to the German war cemetery that was located in a secluded crook at the top of a glacial valley. She insisted we go there. There was a stream nearby where we could sit out on a rock or on the mossy bank with our feet in the fast-flowing bog water. Never mind that it would be too cold.

'It's full of young Germans,' she told us. 'From the war.' Shot-downs and washed-ups, she called them.

Peter wasn't much impressed. He just thought it was spooky. That didn't matter to Kate. She was on a sacred mission.

It didn't matter either that she knew none of the dead. They still counted among her lovely boys.

It was a small cemetery cut into the mountainside, with the graves gently fanning out in the lee of the rock face. There was no one else there. As Kate moved from headstone to headstone I took Peter aside. We would talk about Kate's condition, but first I needed to draw him out. It was contentious from the outset –

'You think you can just show up at my office?'

He gave a bitter laugh. 'Yes.'

'And cause a scene?' I'd been told that he had shouted at the receptionist and then the security staff on the door when he was told I was not available. He shouted that Harry Fielding was never available. He would only leave the building when I presented myself. He was patiently ejected onto the pavement where he continued his tirade before being moved along by a bobby on the beat. 'What the fuck were you at?' I demanded. 'Why didn't you ring?'

'Ring?' His scathing tone indicated that this was an incredible suggestion.

'Yes. Ring. I would have got a message.'

Now he switched to an impossibly reasonable tone – 'You're such a slippery get I thought it would be better to call in.' His twitching was back.

'Just to introduce yourself as my lunatic brother?' He hated what I did. Hated me for spying. It made me untrustworthy. I put others in danger with my cleverness.

He had no idea about my trials in the field. About my knife wound. My going to ground. The cruel state of my relationship with Juno. For one mad moment I wondered if I could just tell him it straight.

No. Of course not.

'The old man visited me in my office,' he said presently.

'Oh yes? And when was this?'

'This was when he was in the home.' There was a formal construct to his words that seemed to assert that if I wasn't guilty of whatever was about to be attributed to me I must be guilty of something else.

I tried to calm myself and to match his formal strain. 'He called to your office? Well now, that's news to me.' He was looking at me hard, and that wasn't like my brother. I wanted to tell him something I had learned in my line of business – that looking at a thing closely can change it in a way you cannot see – but he had already unnerved me. I couldn't trust myself not to run off at the mouth, to range too far and too wide, just as the legs on a stray dog run faster than the animal wants, adding to its confusion.

'He called by at ten thirty one morning,' he continued.

'Seems to run in the family.'

Peter ignored my cutting remark. 'He was wearing his pyjamas under his coat,' he said. 'You could see the pyjamas clearly. He wasn't trying to cover them up.'

'He started shouting, did he?'

'No. But he came up the stairs, not up in the lift.'

'Yes, well, that would have been his new health regime,' I said, glad to be able to show knowledge of his actual condition at the time. 'Every day I went to visit him I found him tramping the grounds, always going up hill if he could.' I was glad to get in the 'every day' reference, because I had done most of the visiting.

My brother was still staring at me but his demeanour had changed again. He was reliving the moment he was describing and it was having a softening effect on him. The twitching was suppressed. 'He just ignored my secretary and walked in with a hearty hello and sat down in front of my desk. In his coat and pyjamas.'

'Did he say whether or not he came by taxi?' I

asked. Now I was looking for details. I was staring back at Peter trying to see what I couldn't see.

'No. He told me he'd walked.'

'That's a hell of a distance.'

'He didn't seem to mind. But I could see he was tired. And I think he was hungry.'

I had a sudden, sharp emotional pang that obviously was to do with our deceased father, but was also to do with Peter and his telling me this story. I didn't know what was going on in his mind, no more than I knew what the dead were doing. I looked up beyond the rock face at the odd assembly of dough-pat clouds. 'Had he been drinking?' I asked. 'I kept him supplied, you know.'

Yes. He knew about my smuggling in whiskey to the old man. How did he know? I had never told him.

'No. He was completely sober. He didn't want tea and biscuits. I offered to take him out for breakfast. He wanted to sit where he was. He wanted to talk.'

'He wanted out of the home?'

'He wanted to talk about you, Harry.' Peter now seemed deeply concerned.

Maybe I had it wrong. Maybe dough-pat clouds were a regular occurrence around here. The old man in his pyjamas going to visit Peter to talk about me – that was definitely an odd event.

I looked down into a patch of peaty stream water. They were there, too. The dough pats.

He saw my surprise. I couldn't conceal it. It was what he was expecting.

'Tell me,' I said, not looking up from the water immediately.

'He seemed to think you were in difficulty,' he said, walking on.

'In difficulty?' What did that mean? I stood a moment in front of one headstone. I could hear Kate reading aloud successive names of her shot-downs and washed-ups with their dates. Peter moved ahead in fits and starts. I caught up with him.

'You were having some kind of crisis . . .'

This didn't sound like the old man. How much of it was Peter inventing for his own satisfaction? A perverse way of feeding his anger.

'As I say,' I mumbled with a kind of forced casualness, 'he was drinking.'

Peter ignored this comment, but rephrased his own. You would think it was me who had turned up in pyjamas. 'He was concerned about your future,' he said. Then, as a *coupe de grace*, he added: 'We all are.'

This sudden, high moral tone of Peter's really irked me. I wanted to get out ahead of him. But I held back. 'That's nice of everybody,' I said. I knew that if I tried to engage him with some reference to my work he would hold up a hand and issue his stock rebuke – you shouldn't be telling me anything. I don't want to know.

I suspect he did want to know. He was being far too responsible. Didn't he remember our very responsible father who, nevertheless, sent us off to school with a pat on the head and a brief to be as naughty as we could?

We lurched on. The ground was firm underfoot. The air was fresh but damp. These conditions seemed to help Peter hold his note of indignation a moment longer before he spoke again. Peter, I wanted to say, never mind your false confusion. Remember as kids you and I broke into our neighbours' houses just to see what they had in their fridges? Remember the buzz we got, and the exotic goodies we stole and ate?

We turned back on ourselves, into another aisle, and as we did so I caught a glimpse of a kingfisher – a vivid blue horizontal flash as it fled from the disturbance we had caused. The old man would have delighted in the sight.

I took the initiative on the subject of family; got on some high ground of my own. I reported one of my exchanges with our father. I acted it out with a few explanatory interjections. I thought it might have his grey hair standing on end –

'The old man: "What's keeping your mother?"'

'Me: "What?"'

'"Where is she?"'

'"She's dead, Cecil."'

'"Yes. Where?"'

'"Dead. You understand dead."'

'This was the third occasion I'd had this conversation with him, Peter. The third occasion he tried to raise her.

'The old man: "Yes. I understand. What's she playing at?"'

'Me: "She died in Muswell Hill. In the house. You found her on the bathroom floor."'

'"Have you no bloody intelligence for me, son? No reliable information?"'

'"She's buried in the Quaker cemetery in Dublin. What's it called? Temple Hill."

'"Yes. I know what it's called, man. Just tell me where is she *NOW*?"

'"She's dead thirty years."

'"That's not – that is NOT . . . are you listening to me?"

'"She was dead on the floor. We never got her to hospital alive."

'"That has nothing to do with me."

'He began to grind his teeth at that point,' I told my brother. 'The old man seemed to think I should know what was keeping her. I fucking told him, didn't I? Told him again. But I couldn't get through. I couldn't get through, Peter.'

I ended the parlour drama there. Or so I thought.

'You could have contacted me about this,' Peter said with a sheepish spasm.

'"*Where's Peter?*" I retorted, mimicking the old man. Mimicking myself. '"*What's keeping Peter?*" You're right. I could have. How stupid of me not to have done so.'

His hair didn't stand on end, but he was troubled enough to break his penetrating stare. What did I want from him, really? To be more like me? Peter had been given the wrong things to rebel against. He had rebelled and become square. He had found safety in being a bore. I, on the other hand, did not rebel. I had continued to be naughty and was expert at, among other things, illegal entry. My insecurities took another form. At our father's funeral I had an urge to reach out and give two knocks with one of the circular handles on the coffin.

'What were these concerns?' I persisted. Kate was

in the far corner now. I could no longer make out the names she was reading out.

'He thought there must be a reason for you drinking heavily. You see, he thought you would be confiding in me.'

'And you put him right?'

'I said I would talk to you.'

'Yes, well . . . I'm not drinking heavily.'

He made an awkward attempt to show a practical brotherly interest. 'You still upset over Juno?'

'Yes, I'm still upset over Juno,' I replied, bristling. I didn't like him using her name. He didn't make it sound right.

'Cecil thought that situation might be affecting your work.'

'Might be making me a bad spook?'

'Personal matters getting in the way of you getting on . . .'

No mention of a lunatic brother ranting in the entrance hall of the MI5 building. I stopped again. I read aloud the name in front of me. I thought if I did that it might concentrate our conversation, take us off the subject of Juno and get us back to the Fielding family conference. I wanted the whole picture, whatever it was. This familial interest came to me as a revelation and would have to be thought through and safely buried.

Trying to explain to your lunatic brother that you're fighting off a nervous breakdown can only be folly. Fact. No explanation needed.

I was being professional. I maintained a professional detachment as we moved on again with a false confidence. I was treating this like an intelligence debriefing. I reminded myself that the danger of being self-obsessed was entirely literal for the spook. It could cost him his life.

I wanted Clements to witness this. You see, Mr Clements, you see how well I'm doing – my presence of mind, my lack of brooding, my drive to understand before my desire to be understood.

'It's beautiful here,' Peter said uncharacteristically. We both stopped and gazed about as though our eyes had opened on this place for the first time.

'Yes, it is.'

He indicated the stream. 'I wonder if there's good fishing further down the valley?'

Peter didn't fish. I took him right back to the old man in his pyjamas. 'Ahh, it's not so strange really . . . Cecil showing up like that,' I said.

'No?'

From the quickness and sharp edge to his voice I realised that he thought the old man might have come to me with worries about him.

'He just wanted to be sure you and I were getting on.'

'Getting on?' he said with suspicion.

'You know . . . talking to each other.'

'Oh . . . right.'

I suggested that later we go to the local pub and raise a glass to Cecil. We had not done so since his death. Though we had no pressing schedule, Peter seemed reluctant.

Back in the car, Aunt Kate took a generous swig from her hip flask.

The tea flask was forgotten. We went for lunch in Enniskerry.

Whatever was going on in his life, Peter's desire to atone ran very much deeper than making up for being a little neglectful towards our aunt.

We were back at the house a short time when I saw him take the mending box from the kitchen cupboard that accommodated Christmas cake and other fermenting goods and kneel down by her easy chair in the living room to sew a button on Kate's antique rose raincoat. We were both able to sew. When our mother became ill the old man showed us how to cook and sew military style. For a moment I watched Kate's arthritic fingers anticipate his work. When Peter caught sight of me in the doorway he suggested he and I go to the pub. He couldn't leave his brother hanging in the wake of what was for us an untypically raw exchange in an odd place.

So, we went. But once we'd ordered our drinks at the bar Peter seemed stuck for something meaningful to say. He was relying on me to lead again and that seemed to choke him all the more. He took a big swallow of rum.

'You're clutching my arm,' he said loftily. 'Why are you clutching me?'

'I'm not clutching you.'

'Am I talking too loud?' he asked, taking hold of my elbow in an iron grip.

'No,' I replied, but he was. He lowered his voice to a conspiratorial whisper. 'You're sure? You'd tell me, wouldn't you?'

I hadn't realised he was quite this drunk.

Yes. I would tell him. I finally saw what was going on – this was *all* about Peter. The clutching gave it away. And sure enough, it came in a gush –

'Things aren't normal with me at the moment, Harry, you see.'

'Och, we all go through' – what did we all go through? I couldn't think of anything on the spot – 'We all go through phases,' I said. He didn't take that well. He must have read the sub-text – you fucking lunatic. 'Christ, you're not dying, are you?'

'No,' he said. 'Not yet.' He released my elbow. What did he mean that things were not normal with him? Was he separating from his wife?

'Thank God for that,' I said. 'You dying – the rest of us would never hear the end of it.'

To my surprise, he laughed at my bad joke. 'Yes,' he boomed. 'But I don't know what's wrong with me really. It's all so bloody . . . so bloody mysterious.'

I agreed that it was. I was in another radio play, I decided. If I didn't get away he'd be coming at me in ever increasing maudlin waves through the rest of the night until he collapsed from drink. I had to escape, but I couldn't deny that I cared about his emotional state. I needed to go somewhere to be alone; to get comfortable again in my own company.

'It's good to see you,' I blabbed, but I meant it.

'Yes. Yes, it is, isn't it,' he replied incongruously. 'I'm on my own, you see,' he continued.

CAVAN COUNTY LIBRARY

A split with Sarah. A complete communications breakdown. Or rather, they had communicated too well and had blown apart. This could all be safely buried if I put a bit of distance between me and my brother. I reminded myself that we had both been drinking.

'Are you?' I said. You really wouldn't think I cared. 'I'm sorry to hear that, Pete.'

'No-no.' He swallowed another mouthful of rum. He put a hand in the air like an evangelist and it was an enormous hand, it seemed to me. 'I'll spare you the details.'

'No, please . . . if you want to talk . . .'

'It's just that it's all so bloody . . . so bloody . . .'

I could see he wasn't going to get the word this time. 'So bloody mysterious,' I said.

He looked at me with a kind of fuzzy astonishment. 'Exactly,' he said. I thought he was going to bring his great hand down heavily on my shoulder, but he didn't. Instead, it came down slowly and went searching for a pocket to rest in. When it couldn't find a pocket it again went for the glass on the counter.

'Now, Harry, what about you? The truth, please.' He was trying hard to show his brotherly concern but it was getting distorted with exaggerated facial expressions. I had not seen these before and I wanted to reach out and smooth them away, but instead, I raised my hand to my mouth –

'I'm better now, Mr Clements,' I lied, whispering into my palm, 'I have made a full recovery and am truly ready for new responsibilities.'

CHAPTER 14

We were going to Sunday Meeting, Kate decided. It would be good for us.

'Oh God,' I protested, 'I don't have to contemplate my sins, do I, Kate?'

'You do,' she replied in a very practical tone.

I went with her to the local shop and picked out a cake. 'That one,' she said, 'it looks home-made.' She dived into her handbag in search of her purse. She gave me the transistor radio she kept in there while she dug into the corners. She found the purse but there was no money in it.

'You couldn't lend your old aunt a few bob, could you, love?'

Of course I could. 'Pity the races aren't on today,' she said as I paid for the cake. 'We could make a day of it.'

I must have inadvertently pulled a sceptical face.

'I don't go on the coach trips,' she said as part of her dissemination of general information designed to let me know that she was still active, still held strong opinions, still spoke up for herself.

'No?'

'They go places in the white vans they use to take prisoners to court or to jail.'

'I see.'

'Powerscourt. Avoca. Places like that. There's usually an off-duty guard doing the driving. The same handsome one. He gets his dinner along with the old crocks.'

'He does, does he?'

'It's coming off a broad board. I told the Gardener he should get a job like that. Better than bending his back all day in the rain. But no.'

'You'd miss your organic vegetables, Kate.'

'Never mind organic. I've vegetables up to my ears.' She shook her head. Let out a little sigh. 'He didn't always do gardening. He used to work in a sweet factory, but the sweets went by too fast, so he quit. Or, was fired.'

I didn't know whether or not to believe her, but it was clear to me she had feelings for this man that went beyond the usual curiosity; the usual indiscretion.

'Peter's looking a bit peaky,' she said. 'I'll have to give him some of my vitamins and – what do you call them . . . ?'

'Supplements.'

'Yes. Supplements. I'll have to give him supplements. I don't want them. I'm up all hours.'

'You watch the late films?'

'I do. It's exhausting, but I still can't sleep. Never mind organic vegetables.' Then she was offering me some of her geriatric nutritional drinks. Pressing them on me. She had plenty. She didn't want them.

She wanted us to have them. Her earnestness upset me.

Peter was more than keen to go to the meeting. I was afraid he was going to create another scene. He got us out and to the meeting-house early. He led us in and chose one of the benches in front of the small wooden table with its bowl of flowers, Bible and decanter filled with water and crowned with a glass that reflected an inverted interior. We sat down and waited for the others to gather. Soon, Peter was staring intently at the great splashes of sunlight on the floor. The ticking of the clock seemed to weigh heavy with him. Rooks called in the surrounding trees, putting out a lame protest at the drone of a single-engine plane that was crawling across the sky. I watched Peter as he fixed on a wasp that took a turn around the room and settled on the flowers in the bowl in front of us. It was late for wasps. That was why it appeared to be drunk. I swallowed this moment of peace, this borrowed stability. Downed it like a bottle of cough mixture.

The Friends gathered, all of them greeting Kate, and making an effort to greet us. Kate responded to each by name.

Peter, I felt, was preparing to make a speech. Something deeply aspirational. A declaration of hope. In my experience a little hope and a lot of hope are indistinguishable.

There was a grumble from Kate's guts. The noise seemed to trigger the beginning of the meeting. Someone spoke about a literacy programme in prisons. Someone else about a programme for fair deals for Third World farmers.

The tyres of a latecomer crunched the gravel. A large, well-preserved man in his sixties entered on spongy feet and took a seat at the back. His eyes sought out Kate. It had to be her gardener. He made a subtle, mildly apologetic greeting which she accepted with an equally subtle nod that seemed to say we must set one clock from another.

Peter did speak. I fixed on the graphic of the running man on the emergency exit sign above the door while he gave thanks for the renewed companionship among family members separated by geography and outlook. Aunt Kate gave me a hard quizzical look. She seemed to think I was responsible or, at any rate, was more knowledgeable than her about this.

Afterwards, over the tea, biscuits and home-made cake, Peter seemed euphoric. He volunteered to take around one of the trays. He felt sufficiently at ease to move the Bible and the decanter to the edge of the table to make room for his tray while he chatted to anyone and everyone.

I was introduced to the Gardener. He gave me the same mildly apologetic greeting he had given Kate. He was cut in half by a shaft of sunlight. He sponged his way in and out of the glare until Kate squeezed his hand, whereupon he made a definite move into the shade.

'Hello, Harold,' he said in a light, round voice. She had told him about me. I could tell. I shook his hand.

'Hello, Bart.' Now he knew she had told me about him. That seemed to come as a relief.

'You're coming to my place for a steak sandwich,' he said. Clearly, he had been prompted because he had started moving again on the spongy feet.

'I'd like that,' I said.

She wouldn't go home in his car. She made him follow behind.

'What do you think of him?' she asked. She wanted to talk about Bart. Wanted approval. She had never done this before with any of her lovers. 'He doesn't say much. Just as well.'

'He's a quiet man, then, yes?' I said approvingly. 'He likes his own company?'

'He has a dog, though you wouldn't know it. You don't see them together. He won't bring it on jobs. The dog doesn't know this is his master. They pass each other as strangers.'

'He must feed it.'

'It has a purple tongue. He puts food down when it's out roaming the streets. The food is just there when it comes back. It doesn't make the connection.'

'It probably likes it that way, too,' I ventured.

'I have an affinity with that dog,' she said.

I tried to show approval for this, too. Belatedly, I wanted everyone in the family to know that Harry was supportive in a pragmatic way. It was the same humility I thought I might demonstrate with the firm, but as yet, it was slow in surfacing.

'He thinks I should put cotton wool in my ears,' she said. '"When it's cold out," he says. Like some of those aul' ones you see.'

'But Kate . . .'

'I'm old, yes – but I don't smell of pee and I don't need cotton wool in my ears.'

'Fair enough.'

'Except when he stays over. When he snores. Let's not talk about me, lovey.'

'Sorry, Kate, but that's exactly why we're here.'

'Oh, bloody Norah,' she cursed, pinching my cheek to break me out of my responsible mode, 'that'll be no fun, will it?' It was quite a firm pinch, and that was a good sign, I decided.

That was when I got the call from Clements. I was to return to London without delay. There was a different class of family business to attend to.

Part 2

CHAPTER 15

We were standing in his office. Was it my imagination or had Clements actually grown taller so that he could be more in character, more usefully clumsy?

I just couldn't get those two words 'fresh' and 'start' to stay together, but, at last, I was about to be fully operational. I was going to be given a brief.

'You're looking well today,' I boomed as though his extra few inches required more volume from me. 'I don't feel so hot today myself.' The indiscretion came out glued to the platitude. It happened that way from time to time. There was a compulsive surge in me.

'Oh?' he said, distractedly. Then, he took a moment to squint into my eyes. I thought he was going to ask me to stick out my tongue. I looked up at the cataract fish-eye light fixture that was in the centre of the ceiling.

My gaze came down in time to catch a brief smile that ebbed and disappeared from Clements's face. Don't ask me about my brother, I wanted to say. Nor about my rogue ex-apprentice or my Judas ex-wife. Don't even ask about my knife wound. Just give me the brief. By all means, something that involves the divining of possibilities, but something concrete. Something that requires a course of action.

He knew I wasn't interested in endless speculation, the relentless posing of hypothetical situations, the paradise of infinity. He knew I was desperate for the job.

Well, I was about to get my brief, and it would set me rocking on my heels.

'How was your trip?' he asked.

'Very good,' I replied, but he wasn't listening.

'You're ready, then?'

Ready for what? 'Yes,' I said.

The agent isn't given much credit for imagination, which I suppose, is fair enough. It's safer that way. The good agent is a resourceful individual. At once an expert in the normal run of things and an oppor-tunist. A resilient coper in the physical world. Somebody with a good instinct for trouble. A good snout. Somebody with a return ticket and a plan of escape. An expert on distance.

Now, did any of that sound like Harry Fielding?

That was my business, wasn't it?

I had been misreading his scrutiny. He wasn't inter-ested in my health. In my state of readiness.

'Have you seen Johnny Weeks?' he asked. The tone of the question begged a confessional reply and seemed to promise immunity of some sort.

'No.'

'He's in London, you know.'

'I didn't know. He said he'd call me if he was in town.'

'Someone tried to run down Jack Bradley last night.'

I left a little pause, then tried to sound callous. It wasn't difficult. 'And we care?'

Clements responded with his own pause. Then he moved to one wall where he stood with his back to me and gazed into a painting. A pastoral scene. A cow in a river. Moss-covered rocks. Ancient trees.

He went to his desk and opened a drawer. He pressed the button on a recorder. Jack Bradley's voice came out of the drawer. A telephone answering service announcement – not at home; leave a message. Then a beep. Then Johnny's voice – 'Jack – you're dead.' Nothing more. Clements stopped the recorder and looked at me directly. 'If Johnny Weeks contacts you, I want to know immediately.'

'Of course, sir.'

He put on his glasses and leaned forward to study some detail in the bottom left-hand corner of the cow painting. 'The realm can't exist by itself,' he said as though he were reading small print from the canvas. 'We are needed. The realm has made us just as surely as it has made the secrets we must keep.'

Though I was thinking big thoughts myself, this philosophical statement seemed at odds with the operational tone. Clements straightened his back again and looked at me to make certain I'd taken in his observation; to ensure that I was basking in the light he had provided for me. The implication was that the same arrangement existed between himself and me.

I was looking at the buttons on the sleeve of my

131

suit, thinking they shouldn't be bunched as they were, one backed up against the next. I was listening but I was on another tack. I was thinking this suit I was wearing, paid for by the firm, was a slave garment. It would have to go.

Emboldened by my truncated period of rest and recuperation in the bosom of the family, I spoke up out of turn, wide of the agenda. I let my impatience show. What exactly was the job that went with this suit? How, exactly was I needed?

Clements was clever about not taking offence. About deliberately misunderstanding when it served a purpose. In this line of work you couldn't fault a man for that, but such knowledge didn't lessen my frustration one jot. I would have to be patient a little longer.

'Didn't I give you the name of my tailor?' he asked.

On the way to his car he gave me the name of a tailor. The firm would pay for something altogether superior. He could see I was fretting about Johnny. He wanted that. His asking about Johnny could only mean trouble. In Johnny's case self-preservation was not a reliable moderating factor. He had come back to London expressly against my instructions. It was too much to expect him to stay drunk and alone in Spain with a desire for revenge eating away at him, but I thought he would have stayed clear until I called him home. In truth, I had it in my head that he would stay clear indefinitely had I instructed him to do so. And maybe he would have had it not been for his own sacred mission.

We were going to court, Clements informed me. The whistle-blower trial.

CHAPTER 16

Time had been consumed with legal procedure and points of law. Not least, the judge had to decide whether or not the case should be held in camera. He had decided in favour of a public trial. And here we were. Clements and me. Concerned citizens. Members of the public. We stood well back from the courtroom entrance. He was watching for someone. He wouldn't say who and I didn't ask. We could hear the buzz from inside. The mill of journalists. The battery of lawyers and court officials. The civil liberties people. Law students. Members of the general public.

I looked up into the hallowed space above our heads. It might have appeared I was gazing up through a column of vultures riding the legal thermals. Clements, I knew, could read my face better. He saw my mind was racing. Where could I locate Johnny? If he was back in London my direct line to him was broken until he made contact. *If* he made contact.

Clements and his kind create their own confederacies that allow for any number of little helpers. And, perhaps, more than one personal assistant. Maybe he wanted Johnny for some dirty work. No. I knew better than to believe that.

Clements spoke with authority when he said there was no such thing as true chaos. There were always people like me in the fray, whatever we might be. Housewife, butcher, painter, spy. We could be exploited. We could be engaged to perform a good deed. For all our individuality we would work to get three ducks up the wall. Insularity was never an issue. Unless, like Johnny, you were going off the rails.

'There is a notion in some quarters,' he turned to me, 'that public service is an old-fashioned idea. You won't find that notion has credence here,' he said, gazing up into the same space as me momentarily. He was still on his broad philosophical beam. I got the impression he was trying to justify something to himself. 'Nor on our patch,' he added.

And that was music to the ears of the irregular duck brigade.

The sense of the service being threadbare and jaded, which these sentiments promoted, only added to our desire to do good. It was all terribly practical, that was the received wisdom. The firm's secret ways were no more mysterious than the private business arrangements of Chinese restaurateurs. And no less successful.

The legendary meanness when it came to Clements paying out from the slush fund for these additional good deeds had a lot to do with integrity, so we were meant to deduce. There was always the vague promise of unbridled generosity, of something exceeding modest riches further down the line. If you stayed on the rails.

'Counsel for the prosecution,' he said, indicating a new arrival.

In the moment, Harry, I told myself. Get in the moment and stay with it. There was a lot of him, this counsel for the prosecution. He carried his fat well. It seemed to serve a purpose. Furthermore, his suit was well cut and slid about his bulk nicely. I watched him as he approached the flight of steps. He swept his arms behind his back like rocket boosters, and made light of climbing the steps. His team had to move fast to keep up with him. He was a little late. He was probably always a little late.

I glanced at my controller's face for an instant. An inscrutable face, yes, but this was a man I was sure gave deep thought to his emotions. Perhaps that was why he was so restrained in their expression. Why he could so easily be labelled a cold fish.

We held back until proceedings began, then quietly made our entrance. Someone was saying that the MI5 smoke machine was at full throttle. Clements stood at the back of the public gallery, all the more solemn, it would appear, for having missed matins. Sorry I'm late he seemed to be transmitting, my truffle pig ran amok in the woods. Sorry I had to bring him with me to these hallowed halls.

I squeezed in behind one shoulder and was able to tilt a few degrees and rest against the wall. Gordon G, the whistle-blower, caught sight of Clements soon after we had entered the chamber. I hadn't met him but his face was familiar from the media coverage. He took in Clements without giving way to any measurable agitation of feeling. That is not to say there was no acknowledgement, for I saw Clements give him the slightest of nods at the moment of contact. I had never seen a nod as slight as this, but it did indeed reach across the room because Gordon G involuntarily returned it.

The MI5 smoke machine remark was coming from our fat prosecutor. His voice wasn't what I expected. I wouldn't have matched the falsetto burr with the bulk. The idea that this so-called smoke machine being at full throttle was, he claimed, an easy metaphor predictably produced by the media and altogether facile when applied to an organ of the realm whose raison d'être clearly demanded a sensible level of secrecy that was always an essential requirement of security. No. Mr Gordon G was a disgruntled man speaking out of turn for his own gain, to satisfy personal grievances, and very much to the detriment of others.

Mr G's resolve seemed more than fortified to me. These opening remarks I predicted would go on for some time. My eyes wandered and picked out a shiny green apple in the upturned hat of a police constable. He was seated at the end of a long bench which ran as far as the dock. The peaked hat with the apple in it was beside him. The defence of the realm was a dirty business, but civil order would prevail as long as policemen ate apples.

I lifted my gaze and fixed on a figure who had just entered and was standing well back. My heart was seized in a pair of cold tongs. Clements drew back a little and spoke, without taking his eyes off the court proceedings.

'I know,' he said, answering my look of dismay, apparently without having looked at me. 'Shocking, isn't it?'

Jack Bradley. Standing in a corner of the public gallery. I couldn't speak. The man prepared to see Johnny and me dead to get his way. The man in my ex-wife. The man who had stuck a short knife in my back.

'It's unavoidable,' Clements said. 'He's needed.'

Furthermore, the man who had sought to discredit Clements. The man who wanted to bring about his downfall. 'I don't want you laying a finger on him. Sorry. It's hard to swallow, I know.'

Bradley was wearing smarter, more conservative clothes than I associated with him. He had grown a beard, which he kept closely trimmed. He was thinner. His bearing more righteous, more judicial. Baptise you sooner than stab you. I detected a false patience. A false humility. A bad piece of work reborn as a bad piece of work. Surely anybody who had any dealings with him saw that.

I wanted to kill him.

He was hanging back in the shadows. The whistle-blower was going to clam up when he saw our Jack, Clements told me in a confidential whisper. The clamming up was essential, he explained. For the greater good. Clements was sorry about that, too. 'Really,' he said, referring to the whistle-blower convincingly, 'I'm on his side. Unacceptable behaviour is just that. But expediency doesn't allow. Not today.'

Suddenly, I found I had been made to promise too much. Funny that, because I couldn't remember promising anything at all, except to keep my mouth shut.

'You want to kill him,' he said. 'I understand.' My

primitive plan sounded better when I had the words spoken to me.

'Another time,' I said.

'That's the spirit.'

The whistle-blower's testimony would compromise some of Jack Bradley's old network of joes, and Jack, who he thought was safely out of the picture, safely discredited, wasn't going to allow it. 'I'll have to stand beside Jack in a minute,' Clements warned with the closest thing to a pained expression he would permit himself. 'You understand?'

'Jack Bradley is rehabilitated?' I asked.

'He's very sorry for what he's done.' Both mousy eyebrows were bearing down to form a straight line. Clements seemed to be suggesting that in the end Bradley wasn't going to get what he wanted. 'But that's none of your business.'

Clements's act of moving to stand beside Bradley was as potent a demonstration of political power as I had seen in all my dealings with the firm. Even before Gordon G saw the two men together Clements had Bradley look across at me and smile.

I smiled right back. That wasn't difficult at all. Then, as both men moved forward from the shadows, I looked to Mr G. I just knew Jack Bradley was smiling at him now.

We sat in Clements's car, parked illegally up a side street. Bradley knew where to come.

'Now,' said Clements as we watched the rehabilitated pretender approach, 'I want you to shake hands.'

It was as if some mild unpleasantness was to be put behind us.

'What?'

'You heard me. He'll like that. Do it, Harry.'

I got out of the car to meet Bradley. He stepped down from the narrow pavement onto the road. I stopped short and let him come to me. And there he was. Right in front of me. I shook his hand. Clements was right. He liked it.

'Harry,' he said with that false humility I'd picked up from across the crowded courtroom, 'I don't know what to say.'

'I understand.'

'I've learned my lesson.'

I nodded, but I wanted to ask what lesson was this? One of Clements's dictums bored through my head – never try to educate. They learn or they don't learn.

'What I'm saying is,' he went on, 'I understand how you feel about me. How it all looks to you.' But we were grown-ups, was the implication. We were older and wiser and evermore bound by our hallowed work. I hadn't let go of his hand. I started shaking it again. He didn't like that.

Suddenly, Clements was out of the car and standing beside us. He put a restraining hand on my claw grip. I let go of Bradley. I had bitten a small nick out of the inside of my lower lip. Only now did I taste the blood.

'Nice to see you again, Jack,' I said.

He came through like a wrecking ball to embrace me. Then, he pushed himself off me with the same force, turned and walked away.

'Mind out,' Clements called after him as a car pulled into the narrow street and proceeded at speed in our direction. Bradley skipped up onto the pavement and raised a grateful hand in the air without looking back. The car sped past us, barely missing our parked vehicle.

'Yes, mind out,' I called after Bradley, but he had already vanished.

Clements and I got back in the car and pulled away sharply into the traffic flow. He was prepared to indulge my incredulity a little longer, that is to say, the denseness that came with the shock of this grubby spectacle I had just been party to.

'It's good we can rely on old Jack,' I whined.

'He's doing his duty protecting his joes.'

'That's all right, then, Mr Clements?' My rage had me asking questions that were completely inappropriate, but I asked, and he answered.

'It's a standing commitment.'

'He's working for the firm again?'

'Yes.'

'We forgive him?'

'Forgiveness doesn't enter into it.'

'You can control him?' I was completely out of line now, but he did not hesitate in replying.

'Yes.'

'But, we know what he's made of.'

'Jack Bradley is a gifted analyst with a formidable memory,' he replied, evidently not entirely convinced by his own words.

'Funny,' I said, 'that doesn't endear him to me.'

'That I can forgive.'

I changed tack. My head was spinning. 'This other material our friend Gordon has,' I said, 'what is it?' There was no capping my indiscretion, but Clements was prepared to continue his indulgence, for a time at any rate. It seemed to serve a purpose. There was, however, a slight pause before he answered. He looked at me directly.

'Some observations on the sacrifice of agents in the field,' he said. 'Allowing bad things to happen.' He wouldn't say any more. At the very least he was referring to Bradley's intention to see Johnny and me killed in the name of his very personal and very unofficial get tough scheme that he had advocated for the service generally when Clements was dethroned and he took the reins.

Evidently, Clements was having to exert a new kind of toughness himself.

Before we reached the pile Clements ordered me not to look so glum. I didn't think I was being glum. I was trying hard to contemplate the greater good, trying to determine what was the appropriate level of bitterness for a man in my predicament. Then he told me I was lucky to get Gordon G's office. There had been stiff competition for it and he had had to assert his authority to get it for me.

Gordon G's office. I let out a strangled, tuneless whinny.

'I'm glad to see it go to a field man,' Clements said.

CHAPTER 17

The doorman asked after my lunatic brother. Everybody in the pile was keen to show that they weren't a conspiracy theorist, but nonetheless were tuned in to the bigger picture. Received wisdom had it that bogus conspiracies were fuelled by 'circumstantial evidence' and therefore were in the highest proof threshold category – unless, of course, we were trying to sell a bogus conspiracy ourselves. It was easy to find yourself mistaking a specific query for a metaphysical conundrum. Particularly if the person you were dealing with had mouse-hair eyebrows.

Despots, Clements said, invariably passed themselves off as heroes. Warriors in the likeness of the disenfranchised citizens they rule. Big and powerful on their behalf. Let others call it a reign of terror. These tyrants were more than willing to undertake the dirty work of purging the enemy within.

'And what do they do, Harry, when they're worried about getting a knife in the back?' He actually waited for an answer, which made me think he was making a less than oblique reference to the wound in my own back.

'What do they do, Mr Clements?' I obliged.

'They organise a coup against themselves to see who rallies to the cause. To see who comes out from under the bed.'

'That's very devious of them, Mr Clements.'

'It is, Harry.'

I was waiting for him to raise his leaden eyelids a fraction and to elaborate with a few inky phrases. I was waiting for the broad-leaf version that would name the enemy. I didn't have to wait long.

'That doesn't sound like our Jack, who was nearly run over, does it?'

I didn't reply, so he volunteered a 'No'. He didn't ask if the generic profile fitted himself. He volunteered that, too. 'It sounds more like what I'm doing,' he said. 'On the surface, that is. If you didn't take a proper look.'

This was not reassuring. Nor did it quell my anger. What kept me sitting on my hands was thinking that I had to get to Johnny. Warn him off. Get him to see sense, for his own sake.

'No, Harry, that would be the wrong end of the stick entirely.'

A short time would elapse before the case for the defence in the whistle-blower trial collapsed and the press had a field day. Gordon G, who had promised to reveal very much more than what had put him in the dock for breech of the Official Secrets Act, would sing dumb. The conspiracy theorists, for once, would be right. Somebody had indeed nobbled

Mr G. Mistakenly believing Jack Bradley had been removed from his position in the firm, he had surfaced and had now been sunk. Gordon would be grubbing up what was legally no defence, that of public interest. His unlawful collecting of information, his lifting of files regarding the alleged illegal activities of the firm, had been suddenly put beyond the reach of his defence lawyers. There would be nothing more on offer.

Staring into the day from Gordon G's office just made me think I needed glasses. I left the building early to send a cryptic message to Johnny via Tina. It was a necessary risk, I had decided. So far as I knew the firm didn't know of Tina. That was one thing Johnny had been very careful about.

I could only wait for him to make contact.

I had a few drinks before I rang Ruth. I wanted to save face. To have her tell me that nothing stood in our way. Instead, we promised each other we would make a date just as soon as there was time. But, for now, neither of us would have time. She was concerned for me in the way Clements was concerned. What I needed to do was to find a nice flat. Perhaps even share. Her plan for me didn't include her as my lover. In the meantime, if there was any emergency we should call each other.

My reconnecting wasn't going too well. Clements could chase Johnny and interview his bomber. His tailor could get cracking on my new suit. I needed to blow my own whistle.

Whichever way I turned my head there it was – my index finger out in front of me, on the end of my straight arm. An extended bleached bone sticking into the dark. I could hear nothing else but that doorbell ringing in my ears. Juno's doorbell.

I didn't know how drunk I was until I tried talking on the telephone. Again. I rang her to warn her I was calling to the house. I knew that if she was there she wouldn't run off. Nor would she agree to my visit. Nor would she turn me away. I covered my drunkenness with my blighted affection.

I had trained myself not to see her again, but I needed her help to do it. I rang from a call box. There was an irate woman who took to banging on the glass. She had a small frame, big hair, white jeans. A poodled-up sixty-year-old with unforgiving eyes. She seemed to think I was taking too long to move on with my life, so I opened the door.

'Do you mind,' I said with my hand over the mouthpiece, 'there's a person in here.' In case she had mistaken me for some other life form.

She moved on. Not because of my declaration, but because I had opened the door with such brute force.

'Who's there with you?' Juno asked.

'Nobody,' I said, but she didn't believe me. She was sure I had an audience. If I wasn't careful I would spoil everything by telling her we should give each other what we could still give. Get hurt one more time.

I took a taxi to the house. I used the journey to get my head straight. I was somewhere between thinking without knowledge and knowing without thinking. I was letting go. Until now I was desperate to learn how it was I had missed her planning to end our marriage. My professional pride had been injured. I should have seen it coming but, in truth, I didn't.

That she would never again seek to confide in me paled when I thought that perhaps I had never been her soul mate, her confidant. That was something else to account for. Something else this selfish spy had missed.

And what made me think I would see more clearly in retrospect? There could be no more learning from Juno at close quarters. No useful observations I could make that would not confuse a man who never knew his own temperature – something hitherto I would have attributed to Johnny and not myself.

No. I was letting go. There could be no 'unless . . .'

I made an effort to insert some emotional distance. I fall out of single beds, I reminded myself. That was a fact. I wasn't bothered by it. I didn't hurt myself when I fell. Usually there was nobody around to see me do it, so I didn't get embarrassed. I didn't know why it happened. I had been doing it since I was a child. It was never linked in my mind with any particular nightmare or dream. I was not wise about it. It never happened in a double bed, even if I didn't get my fair share of the mattress. It was a kind of jaded mystery to me. That's how I felt about this visit to Juno, I decided.

I got out at the end of the street. I felt my face getting bigger. She had come to me like a ghost at my father's funeral and now I would come to her clumsily bouncing off the walls and the ceiling, and making a lot of noise with my big red face.

I passed a drunk several doors up from the house. He was staggering under the weight of the cannon-ball he was carrying in his stomach. The woozy, shocked expression on his face, and his wildly furtive movements poked my imagination – the ball was made of solid gold. Evidently he didn't know how it had got there, but he wasn't giving that much thought. He had to get it home and hide it under his bed without anybody seeing him. Without waking his wife. He would worry about how to discharge it when he got to the top of his creaking staircase. I didn't know whether his tainted good fortune made me feel better or worse, but on I went. Straight to the doorbell with my white-bone finger.

'Where is he, Juno?' I asked.

She knew who I was talking about but she asked anyway.

I was wearing the raincoat she had bought me. A favourite coat that had seen better days. It registered with her when I showed up. It registered, that is, but she tried to ignore the connection.

Well, I wouldn't let her. I held tight.

Later, of course, when I was alone again and I looked at myself in the mirror wearing my favourite raincoat I would see that she had succeeded. I would see that it was shabby and that it no longer had anything of her in it.

I opened the coat now and pulled up my shirt and bared my knife scar. 'Lover boy.' It was a cheap ploy, but it got her attention.

'I don't know. I'm not the one to ask.'

That was a good response. Her words were coming out of an under-heated body. I had thought she would act indignant and ask who did I think I was calling on her in the night like this. But it still seemed like small talk. Words of no consequence. What I was thinking – what I was feeling – didn't get expressed. The words I uttered turned easily in the space between us, deflected by her impatient breath.

'What? You've thrown him over, too?'

'Please, Harry. Leave.'

Now that was more like it. 'No. It's a legitimate question. I'm just getting a clear picture here.'

'Leave me alone, Harry.'

'Let me in, Juno.'

'You're tired,' she said, pretending to make an excuse for me.

'I'm drunk,' I insisted. I didn't mean to say that. I must have been thinking about my cannonball friend.

'Go home,' she said in something just above a whisper.

Was I going to laugh or cry? This was no longer my home. My home was in my tightly cupped hands. And yes, I was tired. Tired of falling behind with her. Tired of trying to activate her voice in my head.

She let me in. She didn't try to keep me in the hall. We went through to the living room. 'Sit down,' she said. But I couldn't sit down. I wouldn't have been able to speak at all if I sat down.

'I've a message for Jack,' I said. 'You give him this.' I gave her a bullet. She was shocked. She let it fall on the floor.

I knew she wouldn't protest. I knew she wouldn't give it to him. I knew so much. I hated to see her lip trembling. It made me shiver.

'I wanted to talk to you,' she said. She could scarcely get the words out.

'Don't call,' I told her. 'And what are you doing closing your eyes when I'm talking to you? Don't do that. Don't do it.'

She opened her eyes slowly. 'How do I contact you?' she asked. I could see she was close to breaking down.

'You don't,' I said.

'If there's an emergency,' she said. I felt for her because she was weary, but these words sounded insincere.

'There won't be,' I said. 'At least, none that I'll be party to.'

'You really are a bastard,' she said.

'Yes. Well, aren't you lucky you spotted that in time and got out – before you got too bitter.'

I pushed my shirt back into my trousers. She looked away. I picked up the bullet and pressed it into her hand. I wanted to tell her that there was no such thing as falling out of love, but I didn't.

It was a short visit. Already, I had done what I had come to the house to do. Though it contra-dicted what I held in my soul to be a fundamental truth, I had confirmed that she had made the right decision to leave me. I had made her believe absolutely in her appraisal of my character and I had done so without telling her that I still loved her. Loving her was my business alone now. Harry Fielding is thorough. Harry Fielding is a finisher.

Now, I had to do something altogether more brave. I had to leave.

I couldn't remember what it was like to make love to her, except in a cartoon sort of way. No more than I could remember the old man's voice, I thought. I could see him lying there in his overgrown garden, one hand twisted around a clump of grass. I could remember perfectly the sounds of the neighbourhood and his silence.

The dead spoke to me while I drove my car or lay on my bed, but they did so using my voice box as their echo chamber. Juno was as dead to me now as the old man, wasn't that my point?

Though she was standing motionless she seemed to be coming at me now like a rotating skydiver, her cheeks suddenly expanded with air, her teeth gritted. I put my arms out to catch her. That stopped her antics. That sucked the air out of her in an instant. I kissed her on the cheek. She moved aside and I made my way to the door.

But, of course, I didn't finish. Not entirely. I relented. It had something to do with being afraid of losing my past with her. I gave her a telephone number. A number that went with a mobile phone I had never used to call anybody and I would never answer. A phone that would be used just once to pick up an emergency message, then ditched.

Love abandoned, not finished.

CHAPTER 18

As predicted, the case for the defence in the whistle-blower trial collapsed. A token case was made for disclosure on the grounds of public interest, but the breech of the Official Secrets Act was established and Gordon G convicted. I would be keeping his office.

Clements summoned me to his house in Oxford that Sunday. I was to inform nobody of our meeting. He was surprisingly clumsy in attempting to pass the instruction off as a quasi-social invitation. Part of his rehabilitation programme for Harry Fielding. There was something vaguely religious about these meetings with Clements. And I sensed he had me marked as an atheist.

In various subtle ways he reminded me of our priorities, our rules, our creed. The sub-text was that I was to break the rules and stretch our creed behind his back, and that I was to do this without his blessing. It had to be without his blessing.

I stepped off the train at Oxford station and nearly tripped over a puppy in a bespoke high-visibility vest. The elderly woman on the other end of the lead was not up to its friskiness and the dog was indifferent to her infirmity. In any case, she blamed me for getting in the way. A superstitious person on his way to meet his boss on a bright Sunday might have taken it as a bad omen.

So, here I was. Answering his call. Tea and buns, Harry, *and* a brief, I thought as I walked down the platform towards the exit, but I had the same creepy feeling I had going to the firm's doctor to get my bill of health.

'If you have any trouble, Harry,' Clements had said of the firm, MI6, Scotland Yard and the entire civil service, 'you can bring me in and, eventually, they'll go away.' Here was an understated assertion of absolute power, and that was compelling. The word 'eventually' he inserted was false modesty. Another of his magnificent general morale-boosting statements that had lodged in my head. Another declaration of confidence in my abilities for which I was meant to feel unworthy. It was working. I felt like a clapped-out chef.

He was waiting for me on the other side of the gate. His grimace of recognition might have suggested that he was there to pick me out from a cash crop of fools, except that he paid no attention whatsoever to the other passengers. He was dressed in his expensive country casual clothes, but something in his demeanour made me think he wanted to be in his suit.

He had summoned me once before to Oxford. It was on his daughter's wedding day and he had urgent business for me. He had taken me to a friend's house. Was he going to do the same again? I wondered. In my limited experience of meetings with Clements outside the office, a trip to Oxford did not bode well for a happy and carefree life.

'I'm lucky,' he said. 'I got a space just outside.'

He had parked his gleaming Land Rover on double yellow lines. You don't see many gleaming Land Rovers, I was thinking as I got in.

'Sorry to call you down at short notice,' he said, 'but something has come up.' He maintained the same locked grimace. I knew he a solution to whatever it was that had come up and that I was to be instrumental in the unsavoury resolution.

'You're in time for a bit of lunch,' he said.

'Good,' I replied. 'I'm hungry.'

I wasn't. In fact, I was suddenly feeling quite sick.

He took us some distance out of the city and forced a little conversation. He had the builders in, he told me. One gable was unsafe. That part of the roof had to come off and a portion of the wall had just been replaced. And weren't we lucky with the weather? More spurious good luck.

We turned by a stand of trees and descended into a flat-bottomed valley that I imagined was a flood plain in spring. Large fields with deep mud tracks. In the centre there was a ramshackle farmhouse with a cluster of outsized sheds with lumpy farm machinery scattered about. To my inexpert eyes most of it looked beyond use. Clements noted my facial expression.

'One of my neighbours,' he said. 'He won't sell.'

I grunted, as if to recognise the limits of democracy.

We came up onto higher ground into a terrain of

closely cropped hedges, discreet ditches and lush meadows. We passed through parkland gates with their neat green railings. A beautiful Tudor hall came into view.

It appeared as deserted as the ramshackle farm. There were no builders, though I saw their scaffolding at one end of the house. Inside, I saw one newly plastered wall. There was a pair of plasterer's stilts in the porch but nobody at home. I got the impression the good people had been ushered out in a hurry. I caught the trace of his wife's perfume in the hallway.

He led me through to the garden and put me sitting on one of a set of outdoor chairs that had been part of the furnishings for the Festival of Britain. When was it? The late 1950s. Clements was rumoured to have a substantial wad of printed serviettes from the same event which he used to help break the ice at dinner parties when he had foreign guests to his house. They could wipe the corners of their mouths with this reassuring memorabilia while there was talk of timely action against emerging threats. I could hear Clements assert that private wealth without public wealth was a dangerous thing. I could hear him declare that old ways may fail but public service was a constant and the realm's only bulwark against an unholy alliance of money, media control and political power. Nothing of quality was wasted in the Britain he served, not even disposable napkins.

'Make yourself at home, Harold,' he said.

I didn't like the sound of that. I was already sitting on one of his festival chairs. What else was I to do? Put my feet up? 'Thank you, Mr Clements.' He went back into the house directly. He must have meant I was to enjoy the garden. Feel free to wander. It was a beautiful garden. Not manicured, more country cottage wilderness. Cornflowers and wild nodding onion plants. Why was I so privileged to be admitted to this inner sanctum? There had to be some kind of emergency. Some secret within a secret. I felt more than usually exploited and nothing sinister had been said yet.

Clements had laid on a gentle breeze. Were it not for the bad feeling I had I could have closed my eyes, lifted my face and let the sun track over me. I could have listened to the birds fly to and from their nests in the eaves. Maybe Clements would lay on a barbecue.

I felt there were eyes watching from other quarters. His family in the bushes at the bottom of the garden, or, perhaps, a minder.

I could see nothing but reflected vegetation and sky in the French windows adjacent. What was he preparing in there? He wasn't pricking sausages.

Then, I remembered – I was 'in time for a bit of lunch'. He was going to produce food after all. He came out with two thick, brown bread ham, cheese, tomato and pickle sandwiches on antique china plates.

'There you are,' he said. 'Best I can do for the moment.'

Hospitality for a parachutist who had landed on his greenhouse.

'Oh, lovely,' I said. 'Thank you.'

Clements was a stickler for manners. Not because he had a heightened sense of social etiquette or because he was a snob. In fact, I suspect social etiquette kept him permanently under cover. It was simply that manners kept confusion at bay. In Clements's invisible dominion where the rightness and the wrongness of conduct was refreshingly free of prescribed good manners he could step out from behind the sun and make bold observations. He could invoke the forces of the Englightenment – reason, nature and wisdom – undiluted.

'Harold,' he said gravely, 'I want to talk to you about Johnny Weeks. The awkward situation he has created.' Clements was a brilliant compartmentaliser. It was difficult to square this with the forces of the Englightenment. Nevertheless, that was his personal quest. His face brightened as a means of punctuating his point came to mind. 'You know that old Russian joke – what doesn't buzz and doesn't go up your arse? Answer: A Russian buzzing-up-your-arse machine.'

I think I laughed. I'm not sure. I looked back through the French windows and took in the ecclesiastical honey light of the interior. It made the environs of the house seem more unworldly, more mysterious. I thought about the plasterer's stilts in the porch. I didn't want to feel what I was feeling.

A short time later he gave me my brief. I was to kill Johnny. He didn't say it outright, but there could be no doubt, that was my task.

'No, no,' Clements said with a positive intonation, and as surely as if he were lecturing with his hands resting on a classroom globe. 'This is the way forward.'

I could think of nothing to say. Initially, I could

process nothing of the information my eyes provided of the face in front of me. I directed my stare at nothing in particular. When I glanced back for a second incredulous take, I found that he had raised an eyebrow, which was a powerful reminder that obstruction by default was not an option.

'Harry,' he said with the birds twittering in our ears, 'you are the man to do this because you understand fully why it is necessary. It is very much appreciated how difficult a task this will be for you. It's a rum business, I admit.'

I think I was meant to turn away from this English praise as though it were in a language I did not comprehend; to go about my duty in a manner that was entirely consistent with British Civil Service practice. He seemed to be saying that it didn't matter what we did if what we did allowed the good citizens of our fair land to enjoy individually what was denied us. Vested in the firm was all the noble humanity any one person could imagine to exist for the benefit of his kind, and maybe a few others, but in a glorious and indivisible abstract.

I couldn't believe what I was hearing.

'Naturally, you take a position on this,' he said.

'A position? Yes. Yes, I do.' My words floated off but were contained in our special outdoor bubble.

'And that deserves a response,' he said with all the rhyme and reason of his office. 'You know what is needed,' he said.

It was as simple as that. He didn't like it. In fact, it made *him* a little sick to utter these words, but nevertheless, they came out with perfect enunciation.

'You know what I want,' he said carefully. As well as my 'knowing what he wanted', he wanted to make it clear that he was taking personal responsibility. Taking it on his conscience. That he wasn't dressing it up. The limits of democracy had surfaced again and had been found wanting, so he had taken me in as a friend and had made me a sandwich.

The action would be forever an absolute secret. We both knew there was no such thing, of course, but that wasn't the point today.

It was clear now why Clements had been so indulgent, so kind as to let me take time to sort family matters when the firm was overstretched. I saw this job had been mine from the moment he had Trevor, or Bryers, or one of the other service monkeys put that note on my hotel pillow. My stomach tightened but I spoke calmly. I was delaying. I was in shock. 'I would want to be sure what you want, wouldn't I?'

He let his eyebrow down gently. He maintained direct eye contact. His inscrutable stare was part of his taking responsibility. I remained calm, but my stomach got tighter. I might have even swayed perceptively on my chair.

'Yes,' he said presently, 'you would.'

'Mr Clements . . .' I said, but he interrupted.

'Harry, you do understand. Be about your business.'

If I had been swaying on my Festival of Britain chair I must have stopped because I was now aware of an absolute stillness that equalled his absolute silence.

We went for a walk in his garden, I think.

CHAPTER 19

I was travelling east on a crowded Central Line train when Johnny tapped me on the shoulder with a banana and moved right into my space. 'Hey, Harry. We're in trouble, right?'

He must have followed me from the pile. Stood by the dragon's mouth.

'Hello, Johnny.' I was glad to see him, but I had an impulse to pull the emergency lever. 'No. I think it's just you.'

He peeled his banana and started eating it, which just doesn't seem right in a crowded train. 'I was afraid of that,' he said with his mouth full. 'How come just me?'

I made a gesture that asked did he really think I was going to talk surrounded by strangers.

'Oh, right . . .' he said, and offered me a bite of his banana. I shook my head very slowly, then glanced at the tube map. I was thinking Baldwin was on Johnny's case, too. They would be looking for him. Clements just had the good sense to know if Johnny trusted anybody, it was me.

Johnny was hungry. He wolfed down the rest of his banana.

'Harry,' he said to make a point of changing the subject, 'I'm amazed to wake up each morning and find that my body still works.'

'You are.' This wasn't a question. I knew he was being earnest.

'Yes. I am.'

'That's a good thing – that you are amazed.'

'I think so. I take nothing for granted. I don't mind saying I learned that from you.'

'You might live longer because you don't.' I couldn't believe these words were coming out of my mouth.

'I will,' he confirmed.

'You're absent without permission,' I said, breaking my own temporary embargo. 'Stay that way.'

'I will,' he repeated in a way that seemed too sophisticated for one who was so angry.

Johnny wasn't a psychopath. Psychopaths don't empathise. They can't read faces. Johnny could read faces. He was just short on doubt. I wanted him to read my face.

'You shouldn't have come back.'

He shrugged.

'I expressly told you not to come until I said it was safe.'

He shrugged again. 'You're looking out for me just as I'm looking out for you,' he said with an easy smile. 'You're a good man, Harry.' He had read my face. He had read the danger.

'Of course I'm a good man.' I wanted to bolt. To be gone.

We got out at the next station. He crossed the platform to a chocolate vending machine and placed his banana skin on top of it. 'We don't want some old lady slipping on that,' he said, 'cracking her head open or taking a tumble onto the live rail.'

'Johnny,' I said, 'you astound me.'

'Do I?' he retorted, the easy smile returning. 'You can't afford to be seen with me. We'll talk.' Suddenly, he was gone. Down a cross passage and up a flight of stairs. I had to chase after him.

Up on the street we set a brisk walking pace.

'There's been meetings about you,' I said, improvising.

'Yes, well,' Johnny said with a sigh that was supposed to represent his new-found worldly maturity. 'There's never a difficulty herding any given bunch of insomniacs into a room at 4.00 a.m., is there? You get them talking. Get them telling each other stories. You just have to promise you'll have them back to their loved ones before they wake. You can't go wrong, can you? You club them up.'

I was clubbed up. That's what he was saying. He had learned a lot from me, but maybe I could learn something from him.

'I'm to be eaten alive by a troupe of monkeys?' he said, returning to the subject of meetings.

Whatever way he said it I could only take it literally. I resisted the impulse to laugh. He didn't often get to make a statement like that. I let it linger.

My plan was to show surprise. To say nothing. To let him talk himself around. He knew I hadn't betrayed him. He needed to vent his anger.

As it turned out, he didn't have much to say. Johnny was never much of a complainer. He didn't think he was articulate enough to do the damage required.

'I don't understand,' he said. It wasn't a flat declaration. It was full of complexity.

'You don't understand what?'

'Why Clements let Bradley away. Let him set us up to be fucking murdered just so Bradley could say I told you so – just to make Bradley look good. Why Clements let the fucker operate knowing he was a threat. When does that get dealt with? Harry, what do you know that you're not telling me?'

'It's down to expediency,' I said. There was no complexity in these words, just a terrible thickness, and he knew it.

'They have a use for him, right? You're going to tell me they've given him a raise?'

'Something like that.'

'It doesn't bother you?'

'Yes, it bothers me.' I was surprised by my own sudden rage, though I shouldn't have been.

'Well that's good to hear.' For a man who possessed many of the monkey tendencies himself, Johnny was curiously trusting, if not evangelical in his indignation.

'Somebody after you?' I asked, sliding my hand over the bump at the small of his back.

'No,' he replied. He locked his spine and made a straight line of his lips to remind himself how he felt – Johnny, you're an angry Buddhist.

'What's the gun for, Johnny?'

'I'm going to shoot somebody.'

'Anybody I know?'

'We know a lot of people who need a good shooting.'

'You're here to kill Bradley. And they know it.'

The killer in him leaned forwards. 'That night,' he said, 'when you found him with your missus – Old Jack wouldn't have got his hand on the bread knife if I was with you. Eah, Harry?'

'It's finished.'

'I would have had him, wouldn't I?'

'Yes. You would have.'

'Never mind,' he said, tapping the glass on his moral compass.

'Never mind . . .' I mimicked bitterly.

'They're going to get rid of me anyway?'

'Yes.'

'Well, thanks for the warning.' He wore his death threat well. I had never seen Johnny more alive, and I had never before felt such an affinity with him.

'Johnny,' I said, 'it's just occurred to me . . .'

'What?'

'You remind me of Jack Bradley.'

'I remind you of Jack Bradley?'

'You know . . . nothing he wouldn't do to get his way.'

He was outraged. He turned his indignant question into a triumphant statement. 'I remind you of Jack Bradley because of what he tried to do to *both* of us. Because I know he fucks your darling ex-wife. Because I know you didn't kill the fucker and now we don't know where we are with Mr Jack. And – because I saved your life in spite of his best efforts

163

and *that* embarrasses you. And so it should. You *should* be embarrassed.'

'Sorry I mentioned it.'

'Hey, don't be sorry to *me*.'

'All right. I won't.'

'Don't be sorry.'

'I won't. All right?'

'Jack Bradley can be sorry.'

'Jack Bradley.' I nodded.

I had had a few drinks after leaving the pile and the light was not good now, but there was no mistaking his gratitude for my warning. It was expressed with a combination of blushing and sneering, and that wasn't the Johnny I knew. He was afraid, and that was a relief.

I pulled rank. I asserted my experience. 'I don't want you going near any of your old hideaways. I don't care how safe you think it is. Believe me, you won't see them coming.'

'All right,' he said as though, reluctantly, he was doing me a favour. He was trying to grow up. So was I. He felt he should be fearless. I wanted to tell him that he had got that wrong.

'It's got nothing to do with your skills,' I said.

'No,' he replied cockily.

'Or lack of them,' I added. I should have had something to eat with my few drinks. I should have got my own banana. I was feeling exposed.

'Can you tell me anything about who has the brief?' he asked.

'They'll kill you. That isn't enough?' He sensed my tightness. He moved in quickly.

'Who will they send? An unlikely pair, yes? An atomic chick with a fifty-year-old taxi driver?'

'If I could give you a description I would, wouldn't I?'

'Miserable as greyhounds,' he said. 'That'll be the giveaway. Doesn't matter how well they've been trained up.'

'And you'd know?' I said, turning on him and thumping him.

For that I got more sneering. No extra colour this time. 'And I hear them click their shoulder blades. They all do that.'

I looked ahead again, gritting my teeth. He wouldn't let go –

'Unless, of course, they send one of the old school. Colonel Chinstrap. You see his type around occasion-ally. Stands in the corner like a toilet brush until it's time to act.' He broke off to take in my irregular stride.

'Are you worried you've been followed? Don't. I've been watching.'

He was making it clear that he was no longer the apprentice. That he was at least as good as me.

He had a point.

He gave me one of those affirmative nods you want to trust, and continued. 'There used to be an old boy like that around our neighbourhood when I was a kid. Brown shoes with the little holes in them, mous-tache, walking stick and driving gloves. He'd take the gloves off to open his bag of boiled sweets. Us kids all got sweets from him. And we got a go of his walking stick.'

I could see Johnny's mind was in fast-forward mode while he was giving me this aside. One of Clements's impromptu lectures bubbled up through the floor of my brain. It was his one on self-reliance – the myth that this was what was wanted in the field agent. A myth that was used as an easy compliment. It meant, in reality, that the agent trusted no one, when what was needed above all else was trust. Trust placed in a controller, that is. What had presented itself to me as a perfectly reasonable assertion, now seemed so obviously hollow and deeply cynical.

Nothing wrong with being alert, quick and evasive in our business. Johnny was all of these things. He was wearing a heavy coat that must have had nerve endings embedded in the fabric that let him sense people behind him. Twice, he turned when passers-by came within range.

On the second occasion he came back to me and said: 'They've sent you, Harry, haven't they?'

What? Me? What are you talking about? Fuck you if you think . . . What do you take me for?

I said none of those things. I just looked at him. It wasn't difficult. I just stared blankly and felt the earth rotate on its axis. I kept my eyes open to keep light in the universe. I began a little nodding motion and that brought more relief.

'That's okay,' he said. 'I know you would have done it by now if you were going to – in spite of being a slow shot. Sorry – does that offend you?'

I stopped nodding. All the sneering had melted away. In place of it Johnny now gave out with a big, unexpected smile. 'Now *you're* in trouble,' he said.

I kept staring at him. The temperature of his smile soon dropped.

'I don't think they trust me to do the job, Johnny,' I said.

What was left of the smile disappeared. He took up my nodding motion and while he did so he glanced over my shoulder twice in one brief moment. He lifted up my hand and shook it. It seemed like a biblical gesture. Something designed to match the Judas kiss he had expected from me.

I caught his hand tightly before he withdrew it. 'You'll have to keep away from Tina,' I said. 'You don't know when they'll be on to her.'

'Yes,' he replied flatly. That was the hardest part to swallow. 'Look,' he added indiscreetly, 'I know what I have to do.'

I didn't believe he would stay away from her.

You did your best, I heard Clements say, speaking out of his nose even before I had released Johnny's hand.

'I said I'd find you – said I'd come after you so they wouldn't send anybody else, all right?' Now *I* was being indiscreet, but a new and more primitive discretion was called for, and I couldn't contain myself. 'But I don't think they believed me. Are you listening?'

I wanted to smack him about. Shake him until his head was bouncing off the wall. I stopped him in his tracks. He was smiling again and wagging his finger as he backed away. Wagging it as if to say – you sly old fox. But really, neither of us felt that smart.

'I'll do what I can,' I blurted out as he slipped into the shadows.

'I know, Harry,' he said, 'you're my friend.' And he was gone.

CHAPTER 20

'Kate, will you look after somebody for me? Just for a short time.'

'I will, dear,' she replied. 'What's her name? Is she up the duff? You don't mind me asking, do you? I mean, I don't care, except –'

'No. It's a friend of mine. He's a colleague.'

'What? Another bloody spy? That won't be much fun for me, will it?'

'You'll like him.'

'What's he done? Buggered the bursar?'

She was as quick as ever. She had picked up immediately that this wasn't a holiday we were talking about. 'No, but you're right. He's in trouble.'

'Well, I suppose that's something. He hasn't killed anybody, has he?'

'No.'

'Your father told me a lot about your antics.' She understood that trying to match what I saw on a map with what I observed around me was a constant. 'What I'm saying is he talked a lot about you when he took a notion to talk to me. What's this bad boy's name?'

'Johnny.'

'Does Johnny do the horses?'

'I don't think so, Kate. Look, maybe he shouldn't stay in your house, but with your friend . . .' I knew the moment that phrase 'your friend' came out of my mouth it was a mistake.

'My friend? Oh, you mean Bart?' She laughed. 'Johnny wouldn't like that, love. Even I wouldn't stay at Bart's house.'

'Johnny's not fussy. I was just thinking – for convenience. He keeps odd hours. I don't want him disturbing you.'

'You mean it would be safer for him?'

'That too,' I said, jumping in too quickly.

'Well, I don't mind anybody disturbing Bart . . .'

'Do you think that would be possible?' I asked, pushing at the same pace because there was no point in beating around the bush.

'I'll ask. I'm sure he'll do it for me. It smells of vinegar, his place,' she warned, 'and the draught under the doors would cut you in half.'

'Johnny's a hardy boy.'

'I wouldn't let *you* stay there.'

'Yes, well, I'm more important, aren't I?'

'You are, love.'

I told her when Johnny could be expected. She would make arrangements with Bart and take Johnny to his vinegary digs.

'He'll pay his way,' I added.

'Oh good,' she said. 'Bart is always looking for a bit of extra cash. He likes to pretend he's lost more than he has when we're at the races.'

'Bart likes the horses?'

170

'He does them to please me.' There was a slight pause, then she said: 'Harold, are you in this trouble, too?'

'No.'

'Good,' she said with an uncharacteristic sigh of relief, 'because I haven't time to hear your story. I'm off to the dentist.'

'Oh, I'm sorry. You should have said.'

'His wife is the assistant. You know when they've been rowing.'

'That doesn't help.'

'Children like to bang on his window.'

'Is he a good dentist?'

'Hah,' she let out loudly. 'I always have a snifter before I go. "You needn't bother smelling my breath," I tell him, "I drove here with one eye closed."'

I let out the same sound. It must run in the family. I knew that she was concerned for this ageing orphan and wanted to ask probing questions, but resisted.

I imagined she would meet Johnny in her broad-brimmed hat, the underside of which was pleated like the underside of a mushroom. She would be wearing too much make-up. And she would make him find his way under the hat to kiss her powdery pink cheek.

'Thank you, Aunt Kate,' I said.

She scoffed.

'Lovey,' she said, 'are you putting Bart in any kind of danger?' There was no trace of suspicion, no hint of reproach in her voice. Nor was she afraid of a truthful answer. She had always been a protector. And she had always been a gambler.

Was that why I felt I could put her at risk? I was relying on her understanding that I wanted to protect him. That I acknowledged there was an element of risk.

I told her Johnny was being hunted. His life was under threat. Telling her made me feel very much worse for exploiting someone who was truly loyal.

'*I'll* take him,' she said. 'He can stay with me.'

'No,' I said. 'It's safer if he stays with a complete stranger.'

There was a pause. Then she said: 'You think I should tell Bart he'll be hiding a man with a death threat?'

I said no again.

'You're right . . .' she said. 'He'd only make a nuisance of himself. Safer not to say.'

There was another brief pause as we both reflected on our souls. She could sense my self-disgust so she made a mental play of weighing the odds of this venture, but I knew she had already decided. She would do anything for me. She recognised this was an act of faith.

'That's that, then,' Kate said.

'I'm told you've met Johnny Weeks,' Clements said. The intonation indicated that I should be very careful how I answered.

'Trevor told you this?' I asked.

'A straight answer, please, Harry.'

'I don't want to work with Trevor, Mr Clements,' I said. 'There's nothing I can teach him.'

'You're telling me he's a fool?'

'No. I'm not telling you.'

'You met Johnny . . .'

'Yes.'

He looked at me for a long time. Then he nodded. 'You'll be meeting again?'

'Yes.'

'Good.'

And that was nearly the end of our conversation. I had been too intent on reading this man, I decided. Not observant enough. It was time to wake up.

'By the way,' he said, 'your brother has been in again.' He gave me a mildly reproachful look that was meant to cut me to the quick. I was supposed to have capped that trouble.

'Was he, Mr Clements? I'm sorry about that. I'm getting him sorted.'

There was a slight delay before he nodded. 'Just passing on the information,' he said with a chilly vagueness.

CHAPTER 21

On the day Gordon G appeared before the judge for sentencing he wasn't wearing a tie. Otherwise, he was as composed and unflinching in his silence as he had been waiting his turn in court before being compromised.

He was sentenced to one year in jail for his car-boot-sale disclosure to the press. It was very much less that the maximum custodial sentence allowed by the law. That had something to do with the measure of material he'd held back.

That same day Clements had made some headway with the bomber. Charlie Bryers dramatised it for me. He wanted to let me know that he had taken my place beside the boss.

This bomber, who had denied all knowledge of the contents of the suitcase he was to 'deliver', had carried no weapon and claimed to know nothing about firearms and explosives. Clements had put a 9mm pistol in a clear plastic evidence bag. He had put it on the table and brought our man in for another interrogation – which went as follows, according to Bryers:

'Sit down, please,' said Clements.

The suspect sat. He tried hard not to glance at the bag on the table, but, inevitably, he did, and when he did Clements leaned forwards slowly with his first question. 'Do you own a 9mm pistol?'

'No.'

'Do you have in your possession a 9mm gun?'

'No.'

'Is that your gun?'

'No.'

'Do you own a gun?'

'No.'

'Have you ever handled a gun?'

'No.'

Clements left a deliberate pause, just to show a bit of patience. He then indicated the gun on the table. 'Have a look at that.'

The suspect had a look.

'Have a closer look.'

The suspect picked up the gun in the plastic, turned it over in his hands and put it back on the table. He made no comment and maintained a stony expression.

'Do you own a 9mm replica pistol?'

'No.' He was thrown by the reference to a replica, but kept to his line of resistance.

'Do you have in your possession a 9mm replica gun?'

'No.'

'Have you any replica guns?'

'No.'

'You're going to tell me you didn't know a replica can be made to shoot. It can be a deadly weapon.' Clements was being a little arch with his 'deadly weapon' assertion, Bryers added, but he was right. It could be made to shoot.

'No.'

'No – you're not going to tell me?'

'No – I didn't know.'

'Have you ever handled a replica gun of any kind?'

'No.'

'Yes you have,' Clements said, lurching forwards suddenly, and jabbing a finger at the gun on the table.

'That's not a replica,' the suspect said with a sigh. He was bored with this game of attrition. But even before he had finished with his sigh he knew he had made a mistake.

'It isn't?' Clements said mildly, leaning back in his chair as slowly as he had leaned forwards in the first instance – another of Bryers's added details. 'That's when Mr Clements looked to me and said "That isn't a replica, Charlie." A primitive trick, wouldn't you say, Harry?'

'Yes,' I agreed.

'But our little bomber was tired.'

There was, however, nothing further to report. No breakthrough. I wanted so badly to be on this job, but I wasn't party to any of this. I chanted this fact to myself. My job was to kill Apprentice John. My champion, Mr Clements, had issued the brief and had explained.

It was the day before Christmas Eve. I rang my brother to tell him to butt out of my life. For his own sake. I couldn't solve his problem. Didn't he know I had no feeling for the waning or, indeed, the strangulation of love? No intelligence. No insight.

I had Johnny to kill. That's what I had.

Peter wanted to see me urgently so I agreed to meet him in a greasy spoon cafeteria near his house. I was there early. I looked around but had no sense of the place, no idea whether or not we should eat there or go somewhere else in the neighbourhood.

'Is the food here any good?' I asked an elderly couple on impulse. They were sitting in a draught by the door when there were plenty of other vacant seats. A bad sign, I thought.

'We've been coming here twenty years,' the old boy said. That was all either of them would say in reply.

I went to the far wall, away from the draught, sat down and unbuttoned my coat. A large booth to myself made me shrink to a comfortable size. I slid along the ribbed red plastic and got myself into cocky lounge mode.

There were people planning murders on the telephone, but I needed something to eat. There was a long room with a tropical fish tank in GCHQ where our 'listening community' might catch wind of other bomb plots. Maybe they could hear the rumbling in my stomach. I might have grown a second mouth just to ask for double helpings of whatever was on offer.

Before I ordered food a middle-aged man wearing large thick glasses and an olive-green gabardine coat entered. He didn't know where to sit. And that seemed to matter judging by his agitated state. He anxiously surveyed the vacant booths. What advantage did he seek?

Now for me there were security issues. The need to have my back to a wall. The need to have a clear view of the entrance. That didn't seem to be the case with him. What was he after? Privacy?

That didn't make much sense given that the place was virtually empty.

Was he worried about light? It was late evening and there was precious little natural light coming in through the windows.

One day soon I would drive myself crazy with this stuff. The poor guy was just a nervous wreck. I should have minded my own business. Instead, I acknowledged him with as much Good Samaritan warmth as you could offer a nervous-nelly stranger. He replied with a tortured twitch.

I saw that he had crumpled paper up one nostril. Things don't go right for a man with paper up his nose. I gave him a second nod.

Maybe I should show him my stab wound, I was thinking. Say nothing, but show him the same measure of warmth as I bared the scar. Maybe that would make him feel more at ease with himself. He might feel some kind of affinity. Or, at the very least, be mesmerised. I just knew he wouldn't feel threatened. In any case, it would be a connection.

He sat down near the old couple by the door. He gave them the same tortured twitch. He rearranged his cutlery. He set up a little rocking motion. He got served before I did. They seemed to know in advance what he would order because the food was out in front of him in double-quick time. Then, quite suddenly, everything was right for him momentarily and we were all happy for him. We went back to ignoring each other, like escaped prisoners from a mass break-out. This was part of the new clarity. The urgent suppression of panic. Me being studiously observant.

When our mother died Peter became withdrawn. A boy sensible beyond his years. He refused to visit her grave, or to travel to Ireland to visit Aunt Kate. When she came to the house in Muswell Hill he would stay out, whatever the weather. True to form, Kate would go looking for him. She would usually find him in the back garden shed, up the lane, or in the park, because, unlike me, he wasn't good at hiding. He never got the hang of looking at potential hiding places from the seeker's point of view.

After one of her visits he went knocking on neighbours' doors asking what our mother was like. He did it systematically. One door after the next. He wouldn't say what they told him. Many of these neighbours had been victims of our break-ins. We knew what they had in their fridges, and now, he needed to know what they could tell him about our mother.

I looked at him when he came in and stood for a moment at the table, and I saw the inconsolable boy standing on a neighbour's doorstep patiently waiting for them to answer the door. I had observed one such visit at close quarters. I hid in the bushes just to catch the doorstep encounter. I knew it wasn't something we could do together.

I had chosen to put myself in the way of Aunt Kate's covert searches. She was good at suddenly turning up and pretending that she wasn't really looking for you. Good, but not good enough to fool me. I could pre-empt her. And I could take Peter's share of whatever was going, I thought.

'Oh, there you are,' she would say casually.

'Yes,' I would reply emphatically. 'Here I am. Peter's gone out. He won't be back for ages.'

'Well, then, we'll just have to do something ourselves.'

'We will.' Torn between being glad that Peter was missing out on attention from Kate, and being full of admiration and concern for my brother, I volunteered that he was 'only half an eejit'.

Kate laughed at this. It was a phrase she and my mother both used. I had heard my mother use it about my father.

'That's a stroke of good luck, isn't it?' Kate replied to my observation.

I agreed that it was. It was understood that there was always hope for half an eejit.

Now he was grown up I could give it to him in a whole portion. 'You're a lunatic,' I said as a greeting, 'you know that? I told you not to call to my place of work. Christ, it must run in the family.'

He was surprised. Even hurt. 'I've got a problem, Harry.'

'You do. Don't call. You're determined to embarrass me. Is that what you want?'

More surprise. 'No.'

'What are you standing there for? Sit down.'

He sat. He had come to tell me that everything was all right between himself and his wife. I was not to take anything he had said in Ireland as announcing the end of his marriage. He had a problem, but he was working it out. They weren't staying together for the sake of their daughter. No. They wanted to stay together.

He was anxious that I forget all his concerns on the matter and that we proceed as before. He was glad we had talked. He wanted to keep in closer contact with me. He thought *he* might be of some help to *me*.

In spite of his contrary behaviour in the foyer of the MI5 building I felt close to him.

I watched as he ate his food. There was no twitching, but one leg was bouncing madly on the ball of the foot. He chewed hunks from a steak and kidney pie as though it were the only pleasure he would get in this world, and even then his darting eyes showed that in affairs of the heart there was need for eternal vigilance.

Me watching him eat was part of an ancient order of two that had been established in childhood. As a boy Peter liked to get himself sent to bed on Friday evenings. Fish and chips night. He would have to be fed. Fish and chips were sent up to him on a tray. Our mother would bring it. Peter would ask her questions. He knew she would find it difficult not to engage, but usually, she got in and out quickly.

Peter wouldn't eat off the plate. Instead, he would

slide the fish and chips onto that day's television page of the newspaper which he had stolen from the rack beside the old man's easy chair. Our father was a bright man, a skilled and thorough civil servant whose job had once been to follow the Axis paper trail of stolen assets across Europe, and still, he could not fathom this act of defiance. It seemed to him – and to me, I admit – entirely out of proportion. The fact that it was a repeated practice never served to lessen the shock.

I would sneak upstairs to watch, and to wait for the search for the newspaper to be taken to Peter's bedroom. Peter would eat his food contentedly as though we were perched in the cleft of our favourite climbing tree. No chips were offered to me, and none were expected, for this was not a feast but a protest.

What had become of that rebellious boy? I wondered. Should I ask him? Should I reach across the table now and steal a chip from his plate?

I told him I, too, was glad we talked. That I might have to go away for a while, and would be un-contactable. But, I would call him. That was all he wanted, he said. It was evident he didn't believe I would call. He would be on his own again, knocking on neighbours' doors.

CHAPTER 22

I walked with Peter as far as his house, but didn't go in. We embraced. We had never done such a thing before and it was strangely exhilarating. We broke away cleanly, connected momentarily at the eyes, then I walked down the lane to the mainline station. It was on this tree-lined commuter path that I sensed I was being followed. Trevor, I hoped, not Johnny. I hoped Johnny had heeded my warning and was far away.

The bullet flew over my shoulder, back to the beginning of my day where I was asleep in my bed. There, it missed me wildly because of the curvature of the earth.

Johnny came out from behind a stretch of rotting fence and ran towards me while I was still rocking on my heels. He kept his pistol out. He didn't stop on front of me. He ran right past, on up the incline. He stopped several paces beyond, apparently content that he had seen off whoever or whatever.

'You . . . you . . .' I couldn't get the words out. They fought each other as they congregated in my throat.

'He's gone, Harry,' he said over his shoulder. He

backed towards me now, still keeping his eyes on whatever had fled. 'He's scarpered.'

I listed to one side and sank against a tall disused telegraph pole. I felt its redwood tree texture against my cheek. In my immediate shock trance I looked up beyond the rusty foot irons. The pole had all its china intact. Look, Harry, you wouldn't have noticed that had you not had a bullet whistle past your head.

'Harry, are you all right?' he asked with genuine concern, which could never be taken for granted with Johnny.

My eyes came down from the top of the pole. 'No.'

He baulked at what he took for professional dis-approval. 'Sure, I could have wrapped the chamois around this,' he said holding up the pistol, 'but that would have defeated the purpose.' He took me by the elbow. 'Come with me.'

He led me to his car. He put the gun under his belt. 'What are you snooping around after me for?' I asked.

'I'm helping you,' he said with indignation. Johnny's self-belief railed against my stalling; my breakdown mode.

'You know there's somebody on your tail?'

'Of course I know.'

'Don't get short with me.' I had insulted him, now. He had shot at me, but I had offended him.

'You nearly – nearly fucking killed me.'

'Hey, I fired this gun. And a very good shot it was. You didn't make it easy. Very fucking difficult angle between you and the other bollocks. Who's following you?'

'His name is Trevor. He's another little helper. Christ, Johnny, you don't just — shoot . . .'

'He's your new apprentice?' he interrupted. There was a risible tone now. 'I could tell by his clumsiness he was with the firm.'

I didn't reply. We got into the car. Trevor, I imagined, was scrambling around in the bushes, trying to get a look at us.

There were chaps and there were monkeys. Some monkeys graduated into chaps. For all his plumminess, his speaking in well-formed, whole sentences, his undeniable vicious streak, Trevor wouldn't be graduating because when he wasn't speaking he struck a posture that took the weight out of whatever he had just said or was about to say. Johnny was right about the clumsiness. Trevor was in the bushes now with his body all bent the wrong way, and not realising he was making too much noise. His sort spying on you was one thing; backing you up was quite another.

'What are you doing here?' I demanded of Johnny. 'I told you they're looking for your blood.'

He gave another indignant, 'Hey. I thought if it's safe for Harry it's safe for his pal.'

'Don't get smart with me. I don't want you looking out for me.'

'I hear you.'

'I don't want your help.'

'All right.'

'I've told you this already and you're still here.'

'I want to buy some new clothes on the King's Road and have a sit-down Indian. What about it?'

I raised my fist, but held back.

'I come home and I find an entirely different man to the one I knew in Spain a couple of weeks ago,' he said. We were both looking out for Trevor in the bushes.

'"Harry will square it with Mr Clements," I said to myself.'

'No, he won't,' I growled. 'He can't, you thick. Now – drive.'

'You told him I'm not going to touch Bradley.' Was he mocking or was he deadly in earnest? I couldn't tell. I scoffed.

But before Johnny turned the key in the ignition he shouted: 'Down.' As we both went down several silenced shots came through the back window from close quarters – too close to allow time to turn over the engine and drive away without a second volley at point blank range. We threw open our doors, rolled out and scrambled for the cover of undergrowth that carpeted the railway embankment a few feet from where Johnny had parked. We dived into the bramble-barbed bushes putting some distance between us.

We took off in the direction of the railway line, crouching low, zig-zagging as lightly as we could on our feet. There was a fundamental difference, however, as to our purpose. I wanted out of harm's way. Johnny's move was tactical. We both heaved ourselves over the wire fence about the same time, but he was much further to the right than I had anticipated.

My toes were pushed into the caps of my shoes going down the steep cut to the tracks. In the short length of time it took for Johnny to emerge on the tracks he had made another cracking evasive move.

We high-stepped over the tracks without breaking our sprint. We climbed the far embankment and scrambled over a crumbling cemetery wall where we hid and watched to see if anybody showed themselves.

We watched and waited with only the sound of flimsy vegetation stirring in a light breeze. We were soaking wet. Was there an equally sodden team under the first line of trees on the far embankment waiting for us to make a move? A team? No. One man, I thought. This wasn't Trevor, I was thinking. Was this a killer with a night scope?

Then there was the rumble. A train passed at full throttle, its vibrations, I imagined, contributing minutely to the decomposition of the bodies under our feet. This was the moment to make my move, I thought. But I didn't move. I waited with my unblenching friend.

A crisp packet flew up from the ditch in the wake of the express and tried to board from the rear, smacking the door in a frenzied spin, but it was quickly ejected from the slipstream.

Johnny was equally good at hunting and evading the hunter. He was perfectly still when I looked across at him. His concentration was absolute. It was absolute because he was looking for confrontation. Johnny had a low sensitivity to fear and that had something to do with his having a poor sense of what he should guard against in himself.

I signalled to him that we should stay put. He signalled that he was content to do so. He was on the lookout for some real competition. The seasoned-up rather than a troupe of dull-witted thugs. I had seen him in action. He liked to let the damaged ones – the psychopaths, the cruel, vengeful ones – get close before acting.

I looked at the cobwebs on his shoulder and in his hair. I could see him go safely to ground with Kate's gardener. Bart's house would be a good hideout. Johnny would fit in nicely. He'd like Bart's easy manner, his steak sandwiches, the alien dog. There might even be some gardening work for him. Bart was altogether far too tolerant, too distracted. This was going through my mind as my gaze returned repeatedly to the crumpled crisp packet tumbling about on the tracks.

If anybody was going to get a bullet in the head it was me. I had to instruct myself. Give direct orders from one part of the brain to another, just to follow the rudiments of survival in this situation. Johnny, on the other hand, was just reading what was in front of his eyes.

He had his pistol in one hand, and a rock in the other.

We stayed there for an hour or more. Nothing happened. Nobody advanced on us. Johnny went scouting. Found no one. We did see a police patrol stop by the car and the coppers get out to inspect it. That was when we made our move. We cut across a garden that was full of scavenged lumber and broken glass. We took a circuitous route through suburban streets to what we judged might be safety.

CHAPTER 23

Johnny, of course, was in no doubt. It was a safe destination. It would be a safe journey. It would do me good, he insisted. It would relax me and he could keep an eye on me. After all, people on their own got terribly down at Christmas. His happy tone, I knew, meant he was looking for conflict. I needed to stay close to him until I could get him out of the country. Until I could plant him in Bart's tumbledown house.

The sweet, toxic smell of liquid vinyl filled the car, giving a hard edge to a seductive unreality. Tina was painting her nails on the way to her mother's house. I felt minute particles of the stuff begin to form a gossamer coating on my lungs. It was too cold to keep the window down for any length of time. Besides, I liked it. I hadn't experienced that pungent female smell in a while.

Tina's mother lived in what had been entirely countryside forty or fifty years ago but was now a rural enclave on the edge of the city. She and a few others had refused to sell to the developers and kept their elevated stretch that on the map registered as one contour above the surrounding terrain.

The car struggled going up the sunken lane to the house. It wasn't a steep rise but there was no relief and there were three of us in it with a load of provisions. The margins were soft. We had to keep to the track. The winter light picked out the moss at the bases of the beech trees that were climbing out over the flat-stone walls. There were cold shimmer shadows of branches on their trunks. These mature trees were half as high again as the pale yellow sun. Even before I had stopped the car and stepped out I knew this was a special place with its own centre of gravity.

'It's beautiful,' I said. Initially, Tina didn't seem to know what I was talking about.

'Yes,' she said absently, 'it is, isn't it?'

One slightly used dog, complete with scars and, no doubt, a collection of unlikely adventure stories, came out through a gap in the hedge that marked the boundary between lane and garden. It repositioned its head, locking into the neck like the barrels of a shotgun locking into the breech. That created a straight line from the tip of the animal's lower jaw to its breast bone. Its rigid front legs lifted off the ground with each hoarse bark. Its barking made the tree tops nod. That was its opening gambit. Then it came at us. First the off-side front wheel, then the rear. A dutiful attack rather than a frenzied assault. Tina was glad to see the dog. She wound down her window and shouted:

'There's my brat. Lead on, Geoff. Lead on.'

Geoff took this as criticism and so redoubled his barking and nipping at the tyres.

'On, Geoff,' Johnny echoed, to no effect.

The rush of cold air made Tina give a shivery laugh. I heard two shotgun blasts in the distance. Was it only disgruntled farmers who took their guns out on Christmas Eve? The blasts sounded hollow to my ears. I think he missed. The sharp winter air perhaps had stiffened his fingers and the quick brown fox was away.

Geoff barked louder still and saw us all the way up the track to the gravel in front of the house. Johnny was out first. The dog greeted him as friend, then came around the car to slobber on Tina, the favourite. Then, suddenly, he took off into the garden after a rabbit or a cat.

'Go on, Geoff,' Johnny shouted. 'Get him. Cats. Cats. Cats.'

I stood for a moment to fill my lungs with cold, damp air. The other two went directly to the shambles that was the porch where they pushed open the hall door. It was an old and rambling two-storey cottage the foundations of which seemed to have sunk by half their measure. I could hear hens having a parliamentary debate in an outhouse.

'Come on, Harry.' Tina's voice carried a long way from the interior. 'We can unload later.'

'Coming,' I shouted. It was Christmas, after all.

I heard Tina calling her mother's name.

I entered the house with the idea of home in the back of my head. I was sure Johnny made a similar aspiring connection. In retrospect, I can identify a gentle melancholy, a silence that was an acoustic camouflage that let you blend into the fabric of the place. Clap your hands and the sound was instantly absorbed by the thick walls and low ceilings. However, I could still hear the clucking of hens and that put me in a fatalistic mood. What did hens know about eggs? I wondered.

Nothing matched, not even the yellowing keys on the walnut piano, but nothing was out of place. You could bang on a drum kit or ride a bike down the stairs and not upset the natural order. It would all be absorbed. I could see at a glance that the electrics were a fire hazard.

Putting aside the risk of being burned alive, a deep, restful sleep could be had here, and that was wasted on Johnny who I knew slept on a rope with or without a woman under his arm. Cats, cats, cats, Johnny.

Wherever I slept, I slept in another domain. I think it was in a place very much like this. Though it didn't smell of cinnamon and mulled wine, as this house did now. I had not been here before. Nothing matched and everything belonged, but there was something odd about the positioning of the furniture, as though it had been arranged by removal men. There was no evidence of Tina's deceased father but his absence settled everywhere and extended to the perimeter of the garden. Perhaps that was why the woodwork hadn't been painted for years but was regularly wiped down and had an ancient, dull shine.

The machinery of widowhood ran smoothly in this house. The interior had for me an unaccountable, unresolved familiarity. It was a safe place that was not my own.

Tina's mother did not respond to her daughter's call. She must have been out of earshot.

There were three home-baked children's party cakes on the sideboard, two of which were decorated with hundreds and thousands. Tina scooped excess cream from one with a finger. There was nothing in her mother's fridge, she explained, because her mother ate everything she bought the day she bought it.

'You wouldn't think it to look at her,' she continued lightly. 'She scoffs everything.' She put a hand out to the sideboard. 'She likes fancy cakes. She'll eat one of those by herself. She'll eat whatever is left for her breakfast.'

She was ambivalent about her claim. Her mother was getting away with something that she herself couldn't sustain, but she had a sneaking admiration for her because of it. Tina wanted children in her mother's house. Wanted to conceive under this roof, I imagined, judging by the way she was leading Johnny. Didn't seem to mind that Johnny's dreams were made of rocks. Probably knew that he was unlikely to stay around. She might even have told her mother all of this, I was thinking, judging by the way she called out again for her in a sing-song voice.

Esther, Tina's mother, was a thin, elegant woman used to physical work. She was putting strands of her hair in place when she appeared in the doorway. I thought she might know about animal husbandry, car maintenance, literature and tea plantations in China. Although we were expected, she was flustered at the breaking of her solitude. I just knew she was ahead of her daughter when it came to Tina's single-parent family planning. Several stages beyond acceptance. That is to say, just short of open encouragement.

Johnny, on the other hand, hadn't a clue.

'Come in, come in,' she said in a small, breathless voice. When her daughter had kissed her she steered us through to the kitchen, which was warmer than the rest of the house. 'You must be Harry,' she said. 'I'm Esther.' She shook my hand even as we moved about the kitchen table.

Johnny embraced her in a bear hug which evidently he knew would embarrass her, and touch her.

'Leave her alone, Johnny,' Tina said, sharing her mother's feelings.

Esther pulled away in a busy manner. Johnny sat down to enjoy it all. He told me to sit too. I was surprised by the informality and the warmth of his self-conscious engagement. It ran contrary to what I had privately come to see as some element of Asperger's syndrome; Johnny's pronounced difficulty in reading human emotions. Was it possible to be partially afflicted with such a condition? Could it be partially or intermittently overcome or resisted? I didn't know. In any case, it was heartening to see Johnny connect as he did. I had caught a rare glimpse of boyish hope in him and it made me feel that there was still a chance we might find a way out.

'Oh, yes, please sit down,' Esther said, flushing again, this time because of her forgetfulness. 'You like

Christmas dinner, Harry?' she asked. 'Some people don't,' she added, just to let me know that if I didn't there was no need to lie.

'Oh yes,' I said. 'I do.'

'I was going to do salmon,' she said, 'just for a change . . .'

'I like salmon, too.' I could hear Clements's voice in my head speaking out of turn, thanking God that the Church of England didn't proscribe food as some other religions did.

'But then I remembered that Johnny doesn't like fish,' she said. Johnny shook his head, confirming that this was so. 'And we have to please Johnny,' she said, smiling mischievously at her daughter, who pulled a teenager's scowl. Johnny, swinging on his chair, nodded to confirm that he expected to be pleased.

Esther turned the same smile on Johnny. That stopped him rocking. She asked him to get wood for the fire before he got comfortable. He gladly sprang out of the chair.

When Johnny came back Tina's mother gave us apple and elderflower juice without asking if we wanted any. She chatted about her hens, the turkey, the dog, the parish newsletter which she compiled, the Christmas issue of which had the two centre pages stapled in upside down.

A short time later she gave us a soft, full-bodied red wine, again without asking. Before we got to the mulled wine she told us about her having to break up a fight in the porch of the church. Johnny was immediately engaged. So engaged that he pulled his chair around to face her directly. The fight, however, had been between Geoff and another dog. Something small and fierce. A stray.

'If it was harvest festival there might have been an excuse,' Esther said, painting a picture of bad-tempered pagan pets being blessed, 'but not at Christmas . . .' Moderation and civilised values read the same whichever way one had to turn the pages of a parish newsletter.

Johnny, of course, approved of Geoff's belligerence. Geoff was getting on in years and Johnny admired his spirit. 'Good boy, Geoff,' he declared loudly, though the dog had yet to reappear.

'He got his ear bitten,' Esther informed us in an accepting voice, 'and ever since I haven't been able to get hold of him. He's off down the garden.'

'Good dog, Geoff,' Johnny bellowed. He looked around for the dog but there was still no sign of him.

We took our bulbous glasses to the living room. Through the window I could see there were sea-gulls gliding in great loops above the house trying to be portentous. If they were there to celebrate the season of good cheer with us they would have been wearing scarves around their necks, I decided. But they were just stupid seagulls. I watched as the underside of their wings turned yellow in the winter light, the same light that lit up a red perfume bottle and made a beacon of it at one end of the mantelpiece.

But there was no rush. No panic. Johnny and I were best of friends and Tina was in love with part of him or all of him, I couldn't tell which. Maybe I didn't have to do anything. Maybe I could just walk away across the frost-covered fields early in the morning and leave no tracks. I could pretend I accepted his lie that he would not go after Jack Bradley. I could pretend that leaving Johnny wouldn't be killing Johnny, just as sure as if I had done Clements's bidding.

The Christmas tree was too big for the house. It wouldn't be right if it wasn't too big, I expect. No two plates at the dinner table were the same and they were all large, as were the knives and forks. The spoons were positively enormous.

We ate and we sank like the foundations. I kept looking at Johnny with his girl. He did the right thing and except for some appreciative sighs, ignored me.

Tina's mother didn't study the couple, but she did study me. Look, I wanted to say, it wasn't me who bit your dog's ear. Nevertheless, it was as simple and as peaceful a Christmas Eve as I had known. Even the prodigal dog came in to sleep in front of the fire and Esther got to tend its damaged ear.

CHAPTER 24

Johnny wandered into the living room early on Christmas morning.

'Oh, you're in here,' he said politely, as though we were virtual strangers who might get on if there was time to converse.

'Yes, I am,' I said. I was so polite in my reply I thought I might get the hiccups.

'Am I disturbing you?'

'No-no.'

I was still waiting for the happy tone to turn to aggression. But he had his hands in his pockets, and I had my feet up on the couch. The dog hadn't bothered to lift its head.

'You've lit a fire, I see.'

'Yes. There isn't much draw on the chimney.'

'Well, it's flat calm outside. I think I'm going to do a fry-up for everybody.'

Keeping his hands in his pockets seemed to help him reverse out of the room. He took a little wisp of smoke with him.

'That'll be nice,' I called after him.

We just couldn't get over ourselves and our seasonal good fortune.

I rang Aunt Kate, to confirm that Johnny was coming. 'You've talked to Bart?' That was the way I put it. 'You asked him?'

She had. But there was a complication. She told me that Peter was there with her. He had come on his own. There was trouble at home, she said.

'I see.' I saw all too clearly. It was scarcely two days since I'd seen him last and he had told me everything was rosy.

'He says he's here to look after me,' she said. 'We'll have to watch him, Harold, won't we?'

'Yes. We will, Kate. You want me to talk to him?'

'He's not here, love. He's at Bart's house having a drink.'

My poor lunatic brother now barred the way for Johnny to quickly go to ground in the Gardener's house, or for that matter, the house in Ranelagh. Peter was taking Johnny's place. Taking my own.

'The dog had a go at Peter,' Kate said matter-of-factly. 'Bart's trying to make it up to him.'

'Sorry to hear you're landed with that. Merry Christmas, Kate.'

'Never mind Merry Christmas,' she said. 'Who are *you* with?'

She wanted to know was there a woman. I had a picture of us in the German cemetery in Wicklow. She had stopped by a mass of dark green and yellow and leaned forwards. 'Now,' she had said, sniffing the air, 'smell that.' She was going to make no further comment until I did as I was told.

I leaned forwards and inhaled a sweet, creamy odour.

'Coconut gorse,' she announced.

'Ah yes. Lovely.'

'I don't know anybody else who wouldn't recognise that as gorse,' she said. 'You were never good at your plants and shrubs.'

'Coconut gorse,' I repeated. Now that I looked at it properly I admit it clearly couldn't have be anything else. I wanted more of it. I inhaled deeply. It did me good. It fed something that suddenly was awakened in the middle of my brain.

'Now,' she said again, and in the same tone, 'tell me about the woman you are seeing.' There seemed to be some connection being made between my not knowing the names of plants and shrubs and my affairs with women. This was typical of Kate's gear changes.

'Don't bother humouring me,' she was saying now on the phone.

'No . . . it's just that it's hard to speak on demand about such things.' It was bizarre to be having a conversation such as this with the pressure I was under. With the sense of foreboding. With my having been betrayed by Clements and his new regime of expediency. A betrayal compounded by my own foolish fantasy of regaining control of my life. My getting a fresh start.

'No ballyhoo,' Kate said. 'Start with the facts. Then, I'll ask questions.' Kate could never be accused of being an incurable romantic. She was never one to be swamped in mystery. She was only ever interested in love on the ground.

Unaccountably, the authority of reason seemed to weigh heavily in her favour. I dithered. I was thinking I was no more secure than my brother, Peter. My flight no less panic stricken than his, yet here I was, doing as Clements had ordered. Playing happy families.

Kate decided she would encourage me further. 'You're afraid to tell me. She's a horrible individual? She has purple earlobes?'

'No,' I said. I decided I would have to lie to make it as simple as she required. Bart's dog was sick, I was thinking. Johnny would make an offer to put it down. I'd have to caution him.

'It's all right with me, dear, if you don't want to talk. I'll give you a banana and send you home.'

'I've been seeing this woman on and off . . .' I began. She jumped in again.

'On and off,' she scoffed. 'You do too much with your boots on. It's the copper's wife, isn't it? It's what's-her-name.' She knew I had a soft spot for Ruth. She had got as much out of me before.

'Yes. It's Ruth,' I said. A lie, because I had finished with her, too, as part of my fresh start.

'Well that's been going a while. It's good between you and her, in spite of your on and off business?'

'Yes. It is.' There was the other half of the lie. It hadn't been going a while, except in my head.

'You keep wanting to go back for more? Now, what is she doing to make you feel that?'

'I don't know, Kate.'

'Ah yes, well, that's a good sign. You probably don't need to marry her.' She managed to make this last remark without my being able to take anything from it.

'No. Probably not.'

'Well, I've no advice for you,' she said, 'not yet, anyway. You'll have to keep me posted.'

'I will,' I said, but I had a strong sense of her going to wherever it was I had just been. Her calling me back. Harry, look what you've missed.

'I'm expecting you to visit,' she said. 'Bring anybody you like.'

I said that I would visit her again soon.

I could see no way of concealing from Clements the fact that I wasn't about to fulfil my brief, and no way of painting my encounter with Johnny that would keep me in the clear. Nor could I see a way of preventing Johnny from administering his own justice. I had never seen him more happy than on that quiet, shatterable morning.

'Now,' said Kate. 'Merry Christmas.'

We walked with Tina and her mother to the church for the morning service. We lingered outside, then went wandering the churchyard with the dog. We took in the carol singing, the light in the stained-glass windows and the stillness of the branches.

Johnny told me the dead had all turned over and were swimming through the clay to get back to their loved ones. It would take them fifty years or more to get out under the cemetery wall, but they were indeed swimming. Even the ones who were forgotten or unloved. He could tell by the height of the nettles. Nettles, he maintained, grew tallest in cemeteries. Most of the older cemeteries and churchyards, he said, were three-quarters empty. This was nothing to be alarmed about. It was perfectly natural.

'But it confuses the dogs . . .' I suggested, with a cursory nod in Geoff's direction.

Johnny looked at me with a deep, quizzical gaze. He hadn't thought of that but now that I had brought it up, it made sense. It was a detail he could add to his theory.

'You don't believe me, do you?' he said.

'I don't think it takes that long for them to present themselves in one form or another,' I said. 'And I don't think there's any swimming involved.'

I looked around the churchyard. Made a point of scanning for interlopers. I wanted to scare him. I should have known better. Johnny began to hum the Christmas carol that we could hear being sung in church. I closed my fists.

Early St Stephen's Day, Johnny and I went for another walk, this time entirely by ourselves. We drove to the nearest coastal town and walked on the sea front. A lot of people had been given a baby in a pram for Christmas. Johnny seemed even more responsible, more relaxed than the previous morning, and that was maddening. He was wearing gloves that were several sizes too big for him.

They flattened his hands into squared-off flippers. Apparently, he was content to rest his digits. He walked with the backs of his hands facing forwards, hands that hung limply, which had the effect of elongating the arms.

We hadn't dared walk the promenade together in Spain, yet here we were, Johnny being reckless and me with my mission to kill or save him. I had learned long ago that chance came before hope in his book. I was surprised how far I went with him.

'I know what you want to say,' he said.

I took a swing at him right there. We were both surprised that it connected with the side of Johnny's head. It was my way of introducing the new expediency. He took it because it was coming from his old mentor. 'Are you listening now?'

'Yes, I'm listening,' he replied with a little shudder to bring on the pain and get his head up to speed.

I gave him facts. Then I tried to explain. I told him about Bradley's agents, the threat of exposure, the gagging of the whistle-blower. After a long silence, he just gave a painful shrug. I was behaving like Clements, showing myself every bit the man for the job with the firm, while Johnny was doing what I had been doing. Except that I wasn't about to carry out my special brief and he was going to kill Bradley.

Johnny went to a corner newsagent where he bought Tina a bunch of yellow roses that were perfectly formed, forced and scentless. It was the best of what was available locally on any St Stephen's Day.

I had a quick look around to see that nobody was watching and I swung at him again. I wanted to knock that innocent expression off his face. He took this second blow as the first. 'Don't fucking do that,' he said this time as he gave another little shudder.

'You're still not listening,' I said through my teeth.

'I am,' he insisted.

He sprayed the roses with his deodorant when we got back to the house. I know this is what he did because, later, he told me so. He knew he was on to a good thing with this gesture. He knew she would like it. Furthermore, yellow was her favourite colour.

He swore he wouldn't kill Jack Bradley. He said that I was showing great leadership with my restraint, my responsible attitude to those vulnerable agents of Bradley's still in the field. He swore he would go to ground soon and without a trace. Even I wouldn't be able to find him.

He didn't want to talk about leaving Tina, but he insisted on talking about Juno and me. I let him. I didn't tell him I had been to see her, that I had finally broken with her. Here was a little nugget of reality we could both bite on, a little ritual we could indulge to show that we cared about each other. A way of asserting that we were lucky or we weren't lucky. Timing had nothing to do with it.

'She wants what she doesn't want.'

'I don't follow.'

'She wants from you what she doesn't want, so she can not want it — from *you*.'

'You're saying, she wants what she can't have?'

'No,' Johnny said patiently. 'She wants this: she wants not to get what she wants. Crucially, she wants that from *you*.'

'This sounds like convincing shite to me.'

'It confirms something — it makes her feel she's got good —'

I jumped in there. I wanted to short-circuit the familiar '— instinct. Yes, yes.'

He came back sharply. 'No. Judgement. It confirms her good judgement. She was right about you.'

'Right about me?'

'You're a good man but you don't understand her so you don't connect.'

'I don't?'

'You don't love her — how could you, right, if you don't connect?'

'But I do.'

'You see — this good man is confused. No — she's right about you, which, of course, her being right about you, is really about her. Nothing complicated about that when you look at it like I do.'

'What about her?' I asked. I tried to equal his instructive and intensely annoying patience.

'She's trying to match up what she's got with what she wants. What should she have at this stage in her life, she's asking herself.'

'Well of course she is,' I said, my bogus patience already draining.

'You see,' he said again, 'it's that simple.'

The evangelical zeal my former apprentice was bringing to the mending of my sorry relationship had become very much enhanced in the relatively short time since we'd last spoken of our respective personal affairs over several bottles of red wine in a dark Spanish bar. Too much sun had finally made him innocent again. It had made him a special kind of stupid. Or maybe it was just a temporary thing – the sudden change in temperature had overwhelmed him, but he would readjust.

'You've given this a lot of thought, I see.'

'I have, Harry.'

His literal answer was not reassuring.

'Well thanks, Johnny . . .'

'Oh, but I care.'

'I know you do.'

I pulled him aside before we went back into the house. We both took it that a good apprenticeship allowed for varying emphasis; for the particular skills and the wisdom of the master, and the emerging strengths and weaknesses of the apprentice. But Johnny was no longer my apprentice.

'Bradley,' I blurted out '– don't –'

Before I got the words out Johnny smacked me on the side of the head with his free hand. 'I heard you,' he said. 'I know about your new friends. I understand. I'm a big boy now.'

Tina liked the smell of Johnny's deodorant. She liked the roses smelling of it. Such is love.

CHAPTER 25

Bradley died instantly from two bullets to the head fired by Johnny at close range. The whistle-blower went back to court. Bradley's network of agents would be digging themselves under rocks once news reached them of their controller's demise. My brother rang from Dublin to leave a message with the doorman at the MI5 building, and that message was: Happy Christmas, Harry. I was sure he had asked the security staff on the door about me just as he had asked our neighbours in Muswell Hill all those years ago about our dead mother.

Clements, I imagined, was quelling his conscience over having to employ the very means he had deplored to see the good people safe. Quelling it in his Oxford garden and being ever more patient but persistent with his pet bomber.

The weather forecast for Spain indicated that it was exceptionally warm in much of the country for the time of year.

Part 3

CHAPTER 26

The lines around each person seemed darker, and they more vivid. Mine was a peculiar waking. Had I really set my heart to right? I was that reasonable, mild-mannered man I was in all my short, slip fanbelt dreams, which were the only dreams I could recall.

The disaffected spy can only aspire to a degree of safety that judges risk to be of an appropriate magnitude and order. He's apt to get reckless. The recklessness comes from a longing for something that is now unattainable. I take my chances, he says, knowing that nobody is listening but his enemy. He makes a point of radically altering some patterns of existence but not others – to equal effect, he hopes. He gambles and tells himself he's playing smart.

The taxi driver approached with his head canted on his shoulders, as if he were judging the path ahead with the better of his two bad eyes. He seemed to think I had beckoned him.

'No, *gracias*.' I wasn't going into the city. I was going in the opposite direction.

'Twenty-five euro,' he said in English. He was

thinking I was tight with my cash. This was a fair price, he was telling me.

'No. *Gracias.*'

He wasn't too upset because he quickly saw another fare when he repositioned his head and, apparently, switched to his other eye.

It was overcast and very close. I stood for a moment, light-headed and sluggish, but looking to mark the beginning of the new phase. The notion I had of being a refugee had to be dispelled.

In spite of it being overcast I was thinking about my rented accommodation; imagining a breeze coming in from the sea, and being able to observe from my bed clotted clouds piled up in the next postal district. I could see a cheap whiskey glass positioned on the ledge of my balcony for the sun to drop into in nine hours' time. That lizard still in its spot, by the way, my new apprentice was waiting for instruction in a civil, heterogeneous life.

Dwelling on my return to Spain was bound to make me jumpy. I needed to iron a few shirts, put something in that glass on the balcony, and get out walking. There was a lot to forget, and I couldn't be using sheepdogs on the green hills of England to fill the gap.

I would belong here for a time, I acknowledged as I filled my lungs with the warm, sea air. Then I would belong someplace else. I was big enough for that. I was lucky to be alive. To be absent without permission, to be missing, to be adrift rather than hunted. Clements, I was sure, was letting me go and that would act as a moral makeweight in his reckoning to do away with Johnny. However, I was mindful that Baldwin might see that as too dangerous and take it upon himself to go after me. Unofficially.

For a moment I literally forgot where I was going from here. I had a complete blank. The void was filled by a deep, quiet, sadness.

Then I became aware of another absence – the constant dull pain in my wound had gone – for now at any rate. That made me think of the healer and his carpet, and then there were thoughts of my friend, Catalina. I would find her. Not say much, just get right into her. I was going to take all that was going and I believed that Catalina would willingly do the same if she had not already committed to a man who might never realise his good fortune. She didn't need to say much either. I could see again how I might belong here. Temporarily. I could see myself shuffling around with my shoelaces undone, making common cause with the ageing dogs of the neighbourhood.

The woody silence I had carried with me surrounded the cluster of sensations that had me looking left and right without knowing which way I should walk.

'Taxi,' said another. This one would do it for twenty.

'No. *Graçias*.'

The weight of my clothes added unreasonably to the weight of my bags. It was too much for my weary skeleton in that moment so I put down the bags, spread my toes in my shoes and stood with my spine at full stretch. There, now, Harry, that can only be of benefit. Like reading good poetry.

I was momentarily rooted to the ground. It wasn't a good spot, but there was no choice in the matter. Someone could come and give me a haircut. I would have liked that. If they could carry me away, so much the better.

I stood there on the pavement outside the airport terminal looking from one weather-beaten palm tree to the next. Was that somebody saying they should call the airport police? Did that cop recognise my shoes from behind his aviation sunglasses? He didn't look friendly. Maybe he had just given up the smokes.

I needed to sleep. I thought about Catalina coming to my room and finding me asleep on my bed and what she might do. I could hear her thinking in her Mexican Spanish.

But I wasn't going back to my flat. Not directly. First, I had another visit to make.

'No. *Graçias*. No taxi.'

Now, where was I lost exactly? There was, of course, no answer to that. No getting back to precise co-ordinates. A person could get frustrated or depressed asking such a question.

Be brave, Harry. Don't trust your feelings here. With just a little encouragement from this Spanish cop you can cut adrift and find again the centre of the flux. The cast-iron container that was my minimum self needed a wetting. A bottle of cold, salty mineral water and I'd be fine.

I could hear the clatter of hooves in a small town square. I got the smell of food drifting up from somewhere below. I could see my cosmic lizard reading with one eye an out-of-date English newspaper on my bed.

A light breeze was enough to blow the cop in my direction.

'*Hola*,' he said sternly.

'*Hola*,' I replied, matching his tone.

A slow grin spread across his face. He must have thought my being rooted to the ground was funny. He said something in Spanish I didn't understand. He might have been asking me if I was here for the elephant polo.

I gave a vowelly grunt. He pointed to my bag and repeated his words. What did he want? Did he want to search my bag? Every cop on the beat in Europe was looking for bombers. I glanced down at the bag and saw that there were clothes trailing out of it.

'Ah – *graçias*.' I stuffed the clothes back into the bag in a deliberately ham-fisted manner and secured the clasp. He didn't seem entirely satisfied with this. The elephant polo was still on. They were short a rider, perhaps.

'Taxi?' he said, pointing lackadaisically.

'No. *Graçias*.' Wrong answer – and I was being altogether too grateful since landing at this airport. I had to make a move. Move, Harry. Move now or the radiation from a previous existence will end it all right here in front of this last sentry.

The cop put his hands on his belt and canted his head in a much more impressive manner than the taxi driver. I thanked him again. I turned the upper portion of my body due west and forced my legs to follow. I made a tremendous effort and began to walk. I never thought I would be grateful to a cop for moving me on, but I was. He held his pose for some time, then collapsed into indifference when he saw me enter the pedestrian walkway that led to the train station.

CHAPTER 27

I gave my face a dry wash. Went at it vigorously. Got into all the nooks and crevices. I took a train to Johnny's town. I needed to satisfy myself that he wasn't sprawled, drunk and asleep and burning up in the sun. I needed to be absolutely sure he wasn't so stupid or self-destructive as to return to an old haunt.

The concierge attached to Johnny's building – I spotted him in a doorway further down, and on the opposite side of the street from where he could keep an eye on his charge. He was talking to another local. A man out shopping for his cured meat, his cigarettes and his wine. I waited until they had finished their conversation and the friend had departed. Johnny's man stayed where he was, casting his proprietorial gaze up and down the street, in a lazy sort of way.

I always think of loafers as being tall figures, light on their feet, who do that dry whistling when they become aware of your attention. They'd be happier in your presence wearing goggles and a snorkel.

But here was a small one. A fresh-faced, tubby, annoying little get with cast-iron feet who liked to think he could call down the slates off a roof to slice a tomato, if he could be bothered.

That suited me. He was our kind of sloth. Undoubtedly a good source of information if you made the right approach, if you won his confidence, and I needed some basic information.

I spoke to him in broken Spanish. He massaged the corners of his mouth with his tongue and let me struggle, but I knew that he was quickly aware of what I was looking for once I nodded in the direction of his building.

The gentleman I was asking about hadn't been home for a long time, he told me, affecting an impressive disinterest.

Yes, I knew that. He was on holidays. But I expected he would have returned by now.

No. He had not.

Had anybody else been looking for him? It was awkward asking a man like this such a question with a put-on casualness, not to say, innocence.

The tongue agitation – which had continued in-between his answers – stopped at this point. Evidently it was time for a smoke. He delayed with his answer while he lit up. I think this was his way of telling me that we could talk villain talk. It didn't bother him. But for all of his posturing, he seemed unsure of himself; unsure of his balance, as if he had spent the previous four days standing in a moving wheel-barrow.

'You mean, the police?' he asked after the first puff of blue smoke.

'Anybody,' I said, playing up the coyness.

'Yes,' he replied.

Yes — what? Yes, police?

He shrugged.

Men. Plainclothes police. He shrugged again at his own speculation. I widened my eyes a little to encourage him. I backed that with a fifty-euro note which I had neatly folded between index and fore-finger before approaching him. I now flicked this with my thumb.

'Customs,' he added vaguely. Did he realise that one of his legs was getting fidgety? 'Or maybe health inspectors,' he added further, presumably just to entertain me.

'Spanish . . . or . . . ?' I didn't finish. But he just looked at me blankly. 'English?'

He shrugged a third time, but answered as he did so. Not Spanish. Though one spoke good Spanish. Much better than me.

He grinned.

'So, they called for my friend, found he wasn't at home, so they came and talked to you?'

Yes. That was what they did. I could see he reck-oned I was in serious trouble because I was doing it the other way round. I was talking to him before knocking on the door.

How many men?

Two.

'And — ?' I said, darting my eyes over both my shoulders. He was flattered that I credited him with being streetwise.

'Two more in a car. A white Mercedes.'

'And you told them — ?'

'I told them what I tell you. He is away a long time.'

'Nothing else?'

'Nothing.'

'Did they come back?'

Now he moved in a way that could not quite be described as a shrug. He told me that somebody had been in the apartment late one night, searching. 'Robbers, maybe.' It was his turn to be coy.

'You checked?'

He shook his head, but of course he had used his skeleton key.

'Anybody watching the building?'

'Yes, I think so,' he said matter-of-factly, and expelled another great puff of blue smoke. He started again with his tongue in the corners of his mouth. He also did a jaw-stretching thing. The interview, I gathered, was terminated. It was time to hand over the fifty.

I held out the money between my two fingers. I didn't thank him. He liked that. It made him feel part of an unregulated global underworld to which he was sure he belonged.

'Are they there now?' I asked before finally letting go of the bank note.

Yes. The two men that were in the Mercedes, but in a different car now. A green Opel.

I didn't look back. I shook his hand and walked on. I took the first turn on my side of the street.

They had found his bolt-hole, but they hadn't got their man. If they had got him they wouldn't be there.

★   ★   ★

The evening sunlight made a brilliant silver seam of the crack that ran the length of Johnny's top-floor window. It appeared to terminate in the glass beaker with pencils on the window ledge. The beaker was Johnny's 'keep off' signal. His warning to me that he was being watched. I took it that he must have put it out before he left for London as a belated precaution. He had never learned to be cautious other than in the moment and in the end, evidently, not cautious enough. For that I felt some responsibility.

As with my neighbour's house, Johnny's place seemed better than mine. It seemed more, well . . . more integrated. More part of an ancient local fabric. A better place to hide. Cooler, too, with its flagged marble floor.

There was a second way in, I knew. Through an adjacent garden that had high walls and an iron gate that was screened with a dense raffia matting. There were mature trees with dusty yellow bark and dark green leaves. There was a flourishing creeper, and in the centre some lifeless pond surrounded by pebbles on which were two curved love-benches facing each other to form a broken circle.

There was a door at the end of the garden that took you into the side of Johnny's building. I had seen him hide a key for this door.

The gate was locked. I got over the wall when nobody was looking. Up on a bin, then over. There was a nice bit of shade from this outsized lumber on a hot day, but even at night there was a smell I didn't like. I couldn't put a name on the trees, nor could I identify the smell. Mustard dust cut with rotten tropical mulch is how I would describe it. It didn't smell any better under the imitation Turkish moon that hung in the sky. I couldn't see oyster shells opening for such a moon.

I moved carefully around the stone benches. I went to get Johnny's key, but it was gone. I didn't want to go any further. I lost my nerve. What was I doing? I had my new life and it didn't include my fugitive friend. I might have been able to find a way of breaking into his flat without being seen, and would have found what? His laundry. A pile of old newspapers. Certainly no clue as to his whereabouts – if he was still alive.

I wanted to see him safe, but I had gone there because he had lied to me and I was angry, which was proof that I wasn't fit for the job of spying any longer. Alas, proof wasn't needed.

I got out of that garden fast. I was sure nobody saw me.

CHAPTER 28

There would be a breeze from the sea. I was thinking I might wash the bed sheets, and let them drip dry into my neighbour's gazpacho while I lay under the billowing canvas that shaded the front balcony. The evening sun would stay longest in the yellow stalks that bore the seed sacks in the ageing palm tree I could see from my window. I might study those yellow sacks or I might just close my eyes. I was passing the wall of rotisserie chickens with these calming thoughts in my head when I caught sight of Johnny. His figure was reflected in the plate glass window. He was standing on the other side of the narrow street, watching me. He had an English tabloid newspaper under his arm.

'Harry,' he called, 'you would have been a genius if it weren't for the mercury in your teeth.'

He had altered his appearance, but I knew it was him instantly. I'd thought if he ever went to ground he would grow his hair and a beard and put on sandals, but I was wrong. He hadn't gone the hippy route, which would have suited him physically, if not his temperament. My self-confessed angry Buddhist apprentice was turned out in Spanish businessman's attire. He'd had his hair cut and dyed, he was wearing a golfing pullover, expensive navy blue flannels, a pair of those see-through socks and low-cut formal shoes.

Initially, I didn't react. I let him call again. I needed a moment to take in the other figures in the street.

'It's all right, Harry,' he said, approaching. 'I tell you what, though, I was looking for a *Times* but all they had was this.' He slapped me on the chest with his folded tabloid.

'Well, how do you like that?' I said. I wasn't going to say much, and I wasn't going to linger. I kept moving at a slow pace. Talking to the dead or the disappeared, you have to remember to leave them room for their utterances. With ghosts you need to ensure they have space of their own to haunt unchallenged by the rest of us.

It was a moot point because Johnny was smug in his new skin. But could he really sustain it? It was a killing kind of solitude. He had made the changes too severe. He didn't know any better. It would be his undoing because, in the end, his fearlessness didn't allow him to believe in his disguise.

He fell in beside me effortlessly. I adjusted minutely to preserve the elemental distance. The smell of the roasting chickens was following us and curling in my nostrils but I was getting strong wafts of expensive aftershave from Johnny. I smelled it even before he had extended a manicured hand for me to shake. All right, so it didn't come as a complete revelation. Nevertheless, I was glad the smell upset me because I couldn't find the emotions that went with Johnny being alive and well and stinking up the place. His smugness extended to his thinking he could see right through my anger.

'You want a run at it, don't you?' he said with a broad grin.

'What?' I asked. I didn't know what he was talking about.

'Death,' he said, checking for thunder around my head. 'You don't want it coming as a surprise. People get that wrong all the time.'

There was nothing to be said about Jack Bradley's killing, except that Johnny thought I was being a little too righteous here with my strained expression. As a result, his apology for his barefaced lying to me about letting Bradley go had an indignant edge to it – 'I couldn't let you get in the way, Harry,' he said. 'The job wouldn't have got done. Am I right?'

I held my stare. That didn't bother him at all. His eyes were pleading that he was a better person than his actions suggested. Now that really had me charged because I felt the same about myself. I had betrayed Clements and the firm. I had made a moral decision and by doing so had made the realm more accountable, less safe. I heard Clements's voice in the centre of my head warn that such scruples might one day soon make it a little easier for a man with a dirty bomb to succeed with his mission. We are better men than our actions suggest, the tone of Clements's voice indicated.

'Johnny,' I said, 'that's a woman's perfume you're wearing.'

'You don't like it?'

'You want to practise in your bedroom before you come out in the streets smelling like that.'

We strolled on down the street, apparently the best of friends.

'Where should I begin?' he asked casually.

'Close to the end,' I suggested.

'I'm going to get somebody buried with my name on the box.'

'Really . . .'

'Can't get closer to the end than that.'

'That easy?'

'I know, it's paperwork, and I'm not the best at paperwork, but I'll find a way.'

'Why are you telling me?'

'I don't want you upset.' He was still beaming.

'So, you parade around here – in this place? Working up your plan.'

'This is your town, not mine. They've already checked my place.'

'I know. They're still watching. Remember to make an entry in the Births and Deaths column.'

He patted me on the arm, just as he had done before he went off to shoot Bradley.

'Hey, it's good to see me, isn't it?'

'Yes. It is.' I couldn't help smiling too, though I must have thought the corners of my mouth would rip if I didn't make it a slow one. There had been a time when I wanted Apprentice John to grow up, and now he had grown up too fast. But there was something watery about his wisdom. Fortunately, animal instinct is not easily diluted.

'I forgive you, Harry.'

'Do you?' I said in a neutral voice.

'For not telling me sooner about your special assignment. I do. I forgive you because you've been good to me.' He nodded at the valise I was carrying. 'You want me to take that?'

'No, Johnny. You want to go somewhere quiet for a drink?'

'Down here,' he said, and we turned sharply. 'You haven't been to your flat yet, I know. I've been watching.'

'Something wrong?'

'Yes. There's somebody there.'

We had been walking slowly. Now, I made sure we walked even slower. 'You recognise them?'

'No. Some old guy.'

'Just one old man?'

'Granda in a fizz bag.'

'What do you mean?'

'He's been buzzing around the building and doesn't know where he is or what he's at. You want to take a look?'

'When I'm ready.'

'I've been looking out for you, Harry.'

'You have.'

'I have. That's why I'm here. There's no other reason.'

'This old fella . . . is he Spanish, English . . . what?'

'Speaks Catalan. From the country, I think. I've talked to him. You want to dip in here for a drink?' He took me by the elbow and led me through a familiar doorway before I gave an answer. 'Put your bag down. Rest your feet. I've got money to spend.'

The tocsin was sounding in my head. 'You talked to him? That was a foolish thing to do.'

'I was careful.'

My eyes smarted going from the bright sunlight to the dark interior. I saw stars. We were in a tapas bar. It was siesta time and the place was virtually deserted. The butcher, whom I recognised from the premises next door, was getting quietly drunk in the corner instead of being at home with his family.

'Nice little place, this,' Johnny said over the sound of my tocsin.

I knew I could trust his good intentions, but trusting his judgement was another matter and now it felt like I was being lured into a lobster pot.

'One of my favourites,' I replied automatically, as I led the way to the far end of the bar so that we could sit facing the entrance. The chaps were out to kill my poorly costumed friend. Somebody in my flat. There was no way I was going to sit with my back to any door.

'You're taking a lot of chances, Johnny. This isn't being careful.'

'Don't Worry. No one saw me.'

'Don't be sure.' The anger was rising in me. I had thought I just might have had a clean break, but I was foolish myself for daring to speculate as much.

'Speaking of being careful — look at this,' he said, hunting out an article in his newspaper. 'America, right?' he said, setting a broad parameter.

'All right,' I said. 'America.'

'"Man Saves Nephew from Jaws of Shark"' he read. He then paraphrased the article under the headline.

'This seven-year-old is in shallow water, right, and a shark attacks. In jumps the uncle. But the shark already has the kid by the legs. The uncle wrestles the shark and the boy out of the water. A cop happens to be on the scene. The cop shoots the shark and they get the kid back. You can see it?'

'I can see it.'

'The cop shooting a writhing shark with a seven-year-old in its razor teeth on dry land. The uncle still probably trying to prise open its jaws.'

'Yes.'

'Cop Shoots Shark on Dry Land,' Johnny announced, reworking the headline with boyish delight at what he found incredible. 'America, Harry,' he repeated.

Was he telling me he was going there, drawn by this recent example of true frontier spirit? Was he suggesting that I go there too?

'America,' I echoed without inflection, without commitment.

He flicked the paper with the backs of his fingers, showing a fresh appreciation.

My anger was still rising. 'What did you do?' I barked, as though it were still my prerogative to question the application of his training. 'You didn't fucking approach the old man, did you? You didn't just ring the doorbell?'

'He's there by himself. I've been watching him. He stands around as though he owns the entire building, but he doesn't know what he's doing. He's an easy one to approach.'

'Are you sure you haven't seen anybody else?' I asked when we had ordered drinks.

'Harryyy . . .' He gave me a look that said he was insulted by my lack of faith in his craft.

'All right. So there's just the old man. Have you been inside?'

'Yes. He's living there.'

'In my flat.'

'Yes.' He was getting impatient now. His mentor was losing his edge, he was thinking, and perhaps he was right. 'Your stuff is gone. I don't know where. I watched him take three-quarters of an hour to move his favourite chair from the front door up to the flat. He wouldn't let anybody give him a hand. Stubborn old git.'

'What's your take on it?'

'With him? He's just some old fella who gets to live in your flat. But who threw you out? And where's your stuff? I don't know.'

'You just went over and talked to him?' I was over-reacting, but I couldn't suppress it.

'No. He has his coffee in a café around the corner early in the morning, and again in the afternoon. The place you like. The one the tourists don't go into. I talked to him there. He's been put here by his family. He won't live with any of them, so they've set him up on his own by the sea. The daughter lives somewhere near. You'd like him. He's a grumpy old sod. He's not interested in his mater-ial good fortune. I don't think he's much interested in the daughter or the grandchildren either. They're all too full of themselves, he tells me. He's preoc-cupied with the faulty intercom. He's worried about his shaky legs. The shaky legs are a new thing. Oh, and – he's not interested in television. Just wants his newspaper.'

'So, he knows nothing about the previous tenant?'

'No.'

'The rooms were ready to let when he first heard about the place?'

'It looks that way. Did you stop paying rent?'

'No.'

'Dirty business, then,' he said, grinning. 'Want a look at him?'

The butcher and the barman seemed to be grinning at me, too, so I just grinned at everybody and Johnny did the same. He was genuinely happy to see me. I had to recognise he was being his usual fearless self. It was me who was in danger of compromising both of us.

'Let's finish our drinks,' I said.

Johnny glanced at his watch. 'You want to see if he shows up in the café? He did yesterday. He doesn't venture far.'

After our drink we walked to the café tourists didn't frequent. While we walked I tried to think clearly about my situation. Johnny read the rest of his newspaper.

'Huh.'

'What?'

'Unbelievable.'

'What?'

'This article.'

'What?'

'It says here that a surgeon was given a dessert-spoon to perform an operation.'

'Oh yes?'

'No. Seriously. A hip replacement operation.'

I must have been in – what's it – a passive-aggressive argumentative mood. 'Could be just the right shape, a spoon,' I said.

'It could be,' he agreed. 'But that's not the point, is it? He was given a dessertspoon. That's the point.'

'And he used it?'

'No. He threw it across the operating theatre.'

'Might be the perfect shape.'

'Not the point. If it's the perfect shape you can be sure they have a dessertspoon-shaped surgical implement. It's cutbacks, isn't it?'

'You think?'

'It says here he went out and bought his own implement for the job. Bloody disgrace, if you ask me. Cutbacks all around, Harry. You would want to watch it – last in, first out, and all of that.' He narrowed his eyes to add mystery to his wet irony.

'Thanks for your concern, Johnny.'

'You want to read this article?' He seemed to think the bizarre tabloid stories would dispel the air of unreality about our meeting.

'No. You've given me the gist.'

There was a brief silence, then he piped up again in the same annoying tone. 'Still, I suppose when you think about a hip – the ball and socket bit – a dessertspoon makes sense . . . It says the surgeon spent a hundred and fifty quid on the proper surgical implement. Seems an awful lot for something as simple as that.'

'Mmm.'

'I know a surgeon gets well paid and all, but still . . .'

'Leave it alone, Johnny.'
'Are you sure you don't want to have a read?'
'Sure.'

We turned into the street where the café was located. Johnny went in by himself and took a seat where I could see him from the mini supermarket across the street. We were a team again.

CHAPTER 29

As if on cue, a short time later an old man entered and Johnny gave me the nod. I watched as he shuffled about and sat down at a table. Johnny acknowledged him with a salute. The salute was formally returned. I watched while Johnny forced a little conversation. He wanted to speak to the old man again about the sudden change in tenancy. This new encounter, however, was fruitless so he took to quizzing me as we went to take a close look at my old flat.

'Well?' he said.

'Never seen him before.'   .

'What do you think?'

'Not a player. I can't see a connection.'

'I'm good, Harry.'

'Yes. You're good.' I gave him a face that told him I didn't need him to hang around, but he just moved a little more quickly in the direction of the square.

'Harry, why do you think your monkey is so successful?' he asked as we made a thorough job of reconnoitring the flat. To begin with, he wasn't talking about the firm's crew of thugs. 'In nature, like,' he added, just to clarify the point. He wasn't looking for an answer. He was going to furnish that himself. 'You think it's because of his marvellous tail, don't you?'

'I'm not really thinking about it just now, Johnny.'

'Most people think it's because of the tail. But it's not.'

'Really?'

'It's because of his ball and socket wrist joint.'

'You read that somewhere?'

'I saw it on David Attenborough.'

'I didn't see that one.'

'Gibbons and such.'

'Right. And why are you telling me this now?'

'I was thinking about the surgeon operating with the dessertspoon. The hip operation. I've been thinking about that.'

'Don't.'

'No. It's interesting. It makes me think about my body. About evolution. Why the human race thrives.'

'You think about the human race?'

'I do. Usually in the bathroom, or when I'm steaming my brains out on the beach.'

He wasn't kidding.

'That's what separates me from the monkeys in the firm,' he added.

We weren't just talking monkeys here. We were talking about our respective futures. Our strategy for survival.

'By the way,' I said as we approached cautiously from behind the man on the horse, 'your comment about my teeth . . .'

'Yes?'

I made a little beckoning motion with one set of bunched fingers and he duly elaborated – after a fashion: 'I read somewhere that the mercury in your teeth affects your brain.'

However interesting, whether true or false, one day the testing of one of these observations that so fascinated him would lead to his undoing, if only by annoying the wrong person.

But not today. Today he would kill anybody to protect us both and would, in spite of his enquiring mind, ask no questions.

'What do you see?' I asked.

He told me there were two opera singers, as he called them, on a balcony in the far corner of the square.

Were they looking at us?

No. And maybe that was because they weren't watching for us.

'Let's not be reasonable, Johnny.'

'All right,' he boomed with a theatrical perversity. 'Let's not.' He was getting to be more colourful in his new guise.

So, we went into a shop and watched them through the window. If they were part of a surveillance team they were doing a good job.

Johnny pointed to the youngsters in the middle of the square with his thumb. 'Children,' he announced matter-of-factly. 'Never trust them. Children are savages.'

'I know. I went to school with them.'

Our opera singers had gone from the balcony. We had watched long enough. I led the way back into the square. We passed a middle-aged woman with burnt sienna hair and caramel handbag with shoes to match. She clocked us. I gave Johnny a look, just to dispel the tension.

He scoffed. 'Fuck sake, Harry. You're going to get us killed.'

I was getting over the shock of meeting Johnny and Johnny was enjoying the relief he so obviously felt. Ostensibly, he had turned himself inside out to make his new life, whereas I was changing as slowly as a tree redistributed its weight to compensate for a lopped limb.

'Where are you going?' Johnny asked with urgency. I was heading for the main entrance and he was going around the side. 'We can't just walk in. Christ, Harry.'

'I'm with you. Slow down.'

Somebody threw a bale of compressed cardboard boxes out of a shop door. We both jumped. We ignored each other's jumping. Recovered equally in half a stride.

Nothing was out of place that we could tell from our preliminary reconnaissance. If the building was under surveillance we couldn't detect it. I wanted to get in quickly, while the old man was having his coffee. I don't know what I thought I would find, but I wanted to take a quick look.

'I'm going inside,' I mumbled as we veered to one side of the building.

Johnny threw me by being suddenly more cautious. 'Are you sure? We don't need to, do we?'

'I'll only be a minute.'

'They'll have changed the lock.'

As if that was ever a bar.

I put Johnny over by the statue. That way I would be able to see him from the window. If there was something out of order he was simply to get up and walk away.

I cut back, went in by the front door, took the lift to the floor above my own, and came down the flight of stairs quietly. Cooking smells wafted up from the second floor, more pungent than I could ever remember.

I encountered nobody in the common area. In a moment I was standing in my old flat, looking at the old man's favourite chair, a battered thing with the horse-hair stuffing wadded around a central crater.

I don't know how long I stood there. Certainly too long without checking to see if Johnny was still sitting by the statue. I could still turn him in. It would be easy for me to trick him. Even now, the firm was beckoning. Promising that I would be forgiven for my failure to act on my brief. Promising more rehabilitation. More time out with the family.

Standing in this room that I'd thought was mine but was now occupied by a grumpy old man, I finally realised I'd lost the run of things. For all his fool-hardiness, I had seen Johnny read the terrain and clear his mind to the task. I hadn't been able to do that.

I wanted to hear in a whisper that this was a moment of truth, and that from here I could go anywhere. Instead, what I got was Clements speaking out of his nose telling me it was more difficult to imagine the ordinary than the fanciful and that that was the undoing of many a spy.

As I stood with my feet rooted to the floor, looking vacantly about me, it was this ordinariness that was the true test of my sanity and my resolve.

I was thinking I might fail that test when I heard a light tapping and Johnny's voice through the door – 'Harry,' he said, 'that intercom still isn't fixed.'

I removed the small wooden wedge I had put under the door and let him in. 'Are you mad?' I asked as he entered the room.

'You didn't show yourself. What's keeping you, Harry?'

More stupid risks.

'I don't know,' I said. 'Nothing.'

'We both should be gone. Come on.' He saw that I was afflicted by some kind of neurological freeze. He put out a hand. He had a small automatic in his waistband with the safety catch disengaged. He should have known better. I would have to give him a dressing down about that.

'All right,' I think I said.

'Did you get what you want?' he asked. He must have thought I had come back for some secret stash.

'Yes,' I'm sure I said. I let him take me by the arm and lead me out onto the landing.

I was impressed with Johnny's coolness as we waited for the ancient lift to crank its way up the caged shaft, a coolness that stayed for the journey down and beyond. Perhaps he was going to survive, after all. Perhaps it was a mistake to think he would never learn.

As we walked out of the building and along one side of the square he told me he had been talking to Tina. I was aware that he was making it a loose formation of two as we made that protracted walk. He was ready to pull the gun, to swing any direction, to push me to one side.

'Guess what,' he said, and had the gall to wait for me to reply.

'What? You're getting married.'

'No. The mother's hen shed has burned down.' He was being so cool I couldn't see the divide between the two parts of the response.

'Really? What happened?'

'The infra-red lamp she had installed – it shorted and caused a blaze.'

'That's terrible.'

'Geoff raised the alarm. Esther managed to get it out before it spread to the house.'

'Thank God for that. And the hens?'

'She got them out before they were roasted. They all scattered into the garden and the fields beyond with Geoff chasing after them. It's a good job Tina wasn't there at the time. He caught and killed two.'

Johnny looked at me. This was the news from England. We both laughed.

'You saw for yourself, Harry – that lamp she put in . . . it was the Hilton for poultry. I mean, hens don't need that, do they?'

We were approaching the statue. Nobody had shown themselves. Nobody that I could see was taking an interest in us. I took in our mounted metal prince for the last time. It struck me that he was a cruel rider. I reached up and brushed one of the horse's hooves as we passed. Johnny seemed to recognise what I was doing, and that was a wonder.

We could afford to be sorry for Tina's mother, who would have wept over her ordeal. She deserved better than to see her shed go up in flames and her pet hens traumatised or savaged by good old Geoff. Johnny suggested I write her one of my letters.

As we made our way out of the square and up a busy side street he went on to embellish the description of the exploding roof of the shed, and the sudden end of the two hens her dog had dispatched. 'There were sparks flying up over the house,' he told me. 'The beams of the shed burned longest. The stone walls made everything go up in a big fireball into the air, scorching the tree near by.'

'All right,' I said. 'I'll write a letter.'

'For a dog that age, eah . . . ?' He was lost in admiration. 'Took out two hens. Not just the one.'

Talking to Tina as well as showing up here to warn me. It seemed there was no end to the risks Johnny was prepared to take. Perhaps it was still the case that nobody in the service knew about Tina, but it was an unsafe assumption and he knew it.

Having to revise my survival prognosis for Johnny — that's what shook me out of my neurological freeze.

As we moved up the town, taking a circuitous route to the train station, he told me that Tina's mother had interrupted the Reverend's Sunday service address to correct him on the details when he made reference to the incident in drawing the congregation's attention to parish matters.

'No, no, Edwin,' she'd said aloud from her pew, 'the hens were saved. They weren't burned.'

'I stand corrected,' the Reverend Edwin had

replied, 'Esther Gillespie's hens were not burned in the fire.' He had already thanked God for the delivery of Esther and her house.

Geoff, Johnny declared, was no doubt curled up in the church porch having forgotten about his kill. He was happy to let them get on with the next hymn.

'I want you to go and see Tina,' he said. Suddenly, there was an urgency in his voice. The wrench of emotion that he could barely contain had me looking over his shoulder in anticipation of some immediate calamity.

I said that I would. I waited for him to say more, but he just repeated his request. The rest was up to me.

'I will,' I said again, fully aware now of Johnny feeling sick with himself. He could act differently in his new disguise, and that was killing him.

He opened one side of his jacket to expose the pistol in his belt. 'You want this?' he asked encouragingly.

'No.'

He deflected my disapproving glance. He kept the flap of his jacket open longer than was necessary to make his point. 'I can get another. You should take it.'

'No.'

'You like this model,' he persisted.

'No. Thanks, Johnny.'

'I won't be around to look after you,' he said with a good measure of self-mockery.

I didn't reply.

'You could practise.'

I had my own relationship with guns that involved nothing as simple as psychosis, a steely nerve, or lack of scruples. I knew that maximum fire-power meant one bullet one kill. I had a steady hand and I was patient. I was more patient than I had ever been. Stretch that patience far enough and with good grace I might never fire a gun again.

Johnny took a long time to smile. 'All right,' he said cheerily.

'You could get rid of that right away,' I told him.

Being a man attracted to his critics, he positively beamed with pleasure as he shook my hand. 'We'll see,' he said.

We didn't have to wait long for a train. He got on. He wanted me to get on, too, but I stayed on the platform. I had somebody I wanted to see before I disappeared.

'I've saved your life again, Harry,' he said from the open door. 'Aren't I the business?'

'You are, Johnny. And now we're in default.'

He liked the sound of that. Johnny was fearless, which was almost, but not quite, the same as being courageous. His fearlessness didn't need to be stored up. It didn't run on batteries. It was constant. Hence his readiness to act in the moment. Hence his simple and often vague notion of what lay ahead. He could never grasp that a failure of nerve might bring a clearer picture with its own implacable resolve.

'That's that, then,' he said.

'Yes. That's that.'

One moment he was there in the doorway, and the

next, he had vanished. The train began to move. I walked along the platform looking into the carriages. I caught a glimpse of him, then he was gone. His facial expression entirely dispelled my Asperger's theory.

I was quite sure I would never see Apprentice John again.

CHAPTER 30

I could want something and go after it. I could try to get it. But, as my brother and I both had discovered, hope depended on others, and when I closed my eyes this was a lot like hoping.

The disaffected spy is apt to gamble on the least favourable odds in affairs of the heart. I went to see the healer. I wanted to give him a message for Catalina. Spin him a yarn and arrange to meet her. The line around me evidently wasn't at all sharp. My aura was sending a complex signal judging by his immediate reaction.

'Come in. Come in, please.' He brought me through to the living room, stood me in the middle of his loud carpet, then formally shook my hand. 'Harry Fielding. You are well?'

'Yes.' I couldn't tell whether he was surprised by his work on me, or disappointed. He seemed to know I wasn't here for healing. Perhaps that explained his perplexed brow. 'Yes, I am. Thank you very much – I want to say that again. I want you to know I'm well.'

He looked me over closely. His eyes smarted. He

was on to something, some scrag-end detail, but what? I didn't want to know. I'd settle for the work he had already done on me.

'Look, I don't want to take up your time,' I said. 'I'm trying to get a message to Catalina. I've lost her number. I thought maybe you . . .'

He interrupted. His gaze had been travelling down my body but now suddenly came up again. 'You have no address?'

'No. It's silly I know, but . . .'

'I can give you her number.'

'Oh good.'

'Please – turn around.'

I turned. I lifted my shirt without instruction. He made no comment, but I could feel heat in the reconstituted tissue of my wound. Heat from his hand. I looked over my shoulder. Whichever way I twisted it caused me pain, but I could see his hand hovering over the scar.

'It's a miracle, Signor Bonfa.' I was sure it was the wrong thing to say, but he ignored the comment. He also ignored my nervousness and my scepticism. He was busy tapping into other emissions from my fuzzy exterior. The result, however, I could only take to be inconclusive. He rattled off Catalina's number.

'I was hoping you might ring her for me.'

Bizarrely, this seemed to confirm some unsatisfactory strain in my healing. Some bad blockage.

'I ring her?' he asked impatiently.

'Yes.'

'All right,' he said, stretching his neck and turning away. He didn't look for an explanation and I didn't give one. He rang her, I think, because he, too, thought it would help, and this was a relief to me.

'Thank you,' I said again, taking his hand in both of mine. I embarrassed him. He looked away again, but this time not so quickly. He would talk to Catalina about my good fortune and my blockage before he would talk to me about it.

'What do you want me to say?' he asked.

'Please tell her you have a letter for her. Ask her to call to collect it before you leave this afternoon.'

He went to the telephone on the side table. He dialled her number. The grubby little spy in me watched to see if his dialling matched the number he had recited. It did. He spoke to her in quick Spanish with his back to me. He then put me sitting in his kitchen while he attended to his last patient. It was a festival day. He was finishing early.

Catalina stepped through the door a short time later. She was annoyed I had got her there on a false pretext. She was happy to see me, though she didn't say as much. She had work to do but she didn't give a damn. She was going back to Mexico.

We drove up into the mountains in her unreliable, oil-burning pile of junk. We went for a long walk. I set my arms swinging. Felt them get longer as the muscles loosened. Though we would lie down together later, Catalina didn't take my hand. I was all right with that. She spoke mostly in Spanish, a lot about returning to Mexico, so far as I could under-stand. We climbed to a vantage point to watch the fireworks. To see if Mrs Espinosa's son would burn down the town.

'So,' I said, casually mimicking myself, 'you think it's a good time for you to go home?' She stopped, looked me up and down with amusement and spoke in English: 'Harry, you are a fool,' she said.

Whether she was talking generally, or, just reprimanding me for not having brought a hat, I was unsure, but I didn't take exception to her remark. From being a fool, I might go somewhere.

I didn't understand what it was that had let me act with impunity for men like Clements. I could only recognise that I had chosen to act contrary to my brief and instead address some misdirection in the making of Harry Fielding. It would take the familiar form of a journey home to get back what had been lost.

One way or another, we want to transcend ourselves.

For now, I needed to rest. Rest as an animal rests. And then, I would be on my way.